Sometime
like
Apes

by
J C Denham

Grosvenor House
Publishing Limited

Cover and inside illustrations by Frances Bell Illustration © 2014
www.francesbellillustration.com

This book is published by
Grosvenor House Publishing Ltd
28-30 High Street, Guildford, Surrey, GU1 3EL.
www.grosvenorhousepublishing.co.uk

The work is distributed by Denham Publishing LLP.
www.denhampublishing.com

A CIP record for this book
is available from the British Library

ISBN 978-1-78148-881-2

Sometime Like Apes

J C Denham was born in Basildon in 1988. He has worked as a teacher of English since 2011 and now lives in Canterbury, Kent. This is his first book.

Catherine, I wrote this book for you but then it turned out rather dark. Sorry about that. I hope you still like it and thank you for everything.

Thanks, too, to those intrinsic to the inception, creation and publication of this novella: dad, mum, Frances, et al.

1

I grew out of the earth into a night so cold it was sharp and dry like broken glass. I was born of sinuous roots and broken-bone stone, pushed from muscles of mud. I clung and pulled at locks of grass, slipped out of the ground and took my first breath.

Why not?

I learned that the ground I dreamed I came from is called a mire, and that the night belonged to winter.

That's not what he said though, the master, when the spotlight pitched on me in the middle of the tent. When I felt I was frozen and only the gravel spoke for me in low groans and crunches as I shifted about on my soles.

He told a different tale.

'See his resemblance to a fish?'

I look nothing like a fish.

'But with the height of a man? See his scales, see his size. I caught him in the South Pacific, in seas as deep as time. He cried out like the cracken, and snapped his beak just like it too. I beat him down and shackled him, and brought him back for you. I fished him from the ocean, and put him in a cage. I saw him full of evil and I saw him full of rage. If I fed him once I beat him twice, until he saw that he was mine. Until he was but half a man – and half a fish, I think you'll find.'

I'm not a half of anything.

He's sung that song to audiences many times, and I don't remember anything before he started. We drew lines across the world like pens on paper, joined scratched on, soot-sketches of cities. We left nothing but chewed-up, damp fliers and patches of dead grass

Heave-ho, up the cathedral goes. This great big red and white striped tent. Ten men pull it up in the pouring rain, always in the middle of the night. It's always pouring rain in the middle of the night.

'Turn the flood lights on,' they'd scream at me. '*Turn the lights on, Caliban.*'

And I walked and talked and I put up a great big tent every few nights. There isn't a fish I know that can do all that.

'Ladies and Gentleman - if you'll forgive an old man a dreadful cliché - the show is about to start. And not just any show, but the most tantalizing exhibition of human limits; a carnal carnival of the ostentatious, the absurd and the simply unmissable. I hope you have left your imaginations at home, because they could not possibly comprehend the sheer spectacle that I, your master, will lay upon you tonight. This really is *The Greatest Show on Earth.*

'The loving arms of empire have been wrapped half way around this wretched world, and I, your master, have trapped all the wonders in it, just for you. I have been across the latitudes, to a rotting place, and caught the majestic elephant so that you don't have to. I have travelled even farther, kept a deferential face and fought the mighty lion so you can leer, you can sneer, you can even jeer at the king of the jungle himself. Right here. I've crossed the great equator, and with enormous care I've hunted just for you the deadly moon bear.

'And they are all here, in splendid isolation, along with all your favourite acts: We have Pockets and Tick, the queerest clowns in town. We have Ariel and His Spirits, who will defy all science and reason with their feats of daring, their absence of fear in the face of some of the greatest stunts ever attempted.

'And, of course, fresh from my latest sojourn into the deepest and darkest parts of the world, our brand new act, the one I know you have been waiting to see: Caliban, primitive man, the newest edition to our cauldron of curiosities.

'All of this and much, much more awaits you tonight in this very ring. Ladies and Gentlemen, if you please, sit back and enjoy *The Greatest Show on Earth*.'

So here's what happened then – I guess I'll start remembering.

In every charcoal town we visited we pitched ourselves up in an aisle of acts. Tents and huts and cages contained men and beasts – and things in-between.

When I became awake and found that I was there I was shackled at the darkest end of an aisle. There the sawdust thinned, and in the night the wet grass and my cracked skin both shone as one. The aisle appeared a tunnel, the light at the end that great, big, red and white striped tent.

I scanned it like a wild thing.

I clawed at the shackle around my ankle, traced the chains to their source until I was sure, just as before, that they had not loosened.

Sometime I drove my fingers into the ground to uproot a fist of earth in each palm. I brought them together under my nose and breathed. It was foreign, and I buried it back in its place.

I scanned the tent like a wild thing. It pulsed with the sounds of carnival. Laughter, music and applause – all things I'd never heard before – toured the lengthy corridor. They fell on my ears as alien.

This was the first thing the master said to me:

'Would you like to know what makes my little show the greatest one on earth? The fact that my acts simply sparkle more, in the eyes of my audience, than any other. It's the radiance of the thing. When Edison invented his version of the lamp, he was able to better his contemporaries for one simple reason; a more effective incandescent material. His light burned brighter.

'You are our incandescent material, and you will burn brighter than them all,' then he dragged me down the middle of the aisle towards the tent.

'My catalyst,' he said. 'My curiosity, my creature. My Caliban.'

A long time has passed since my first performance. Many seasons. The early one is my favourite, when green leaves are all around, dancing, and long grass moves as one in the wind like an ocean. I only ever saw it from a cage. In my dreams that season bent the bars and slept with me. The long grass and its thousands of tiny arms holding me.

But on that first night:

'Now I'd like to introduce to you, my friends,' said the master, '– I feel we have become friends. After all, we have experienced something very special together tonight, something rather surreal and wonderful – I'd like to introduce to you, dear friends, my favourite moment of the evening, and what an evening it has already been. It's rare that I get an opportunity to offer you a thing no other circus in the world can. I have, as mentioned, travelled the earth for you to bring you these sights, these delights, and this *horror*.'

Sometime we are all forced to march by knives. I was, to the middle of a spotlight, churning gravel under my feet with every tiny step.

The crowd, in a fit of excitement, brought the air in the tent to a boil so thick I struggled, quickly learnt to swim. I clawed and pawed and gnawed at them and only made things worse. They wanted to see a wild thing, and a wild thing I was.

Somewhere there were drums. Pulsing, otherworldly drums rolling through the darkness beyond the spotlight with such a pressure, this aching pressure that goaded the crowd on further.

Coins rained down on me so that I curled up in a ball. My cracked skin with the patches of hair my only shield from the boiling air and the metal hale.

Beyond the limits of the ring came that battery and bawling. I chanced a glance between my fingers but could not see past a black wall the crowd's lash and the stage's lights had put up. There was a glimpse of men, women, of children past the dark foil, perhaps. Their faces were empty. In every show those empty, slate faces. Hollow and eyeless and seeing nonetheless.

Beside me, his eyes always on the crowd, was the master.

'See its scales, see its size! I caught it in the South Pacific, in seas as deep as time'...

The master stood like a soldier-clown in a red, brass buttoned jacket and white trousers. Stiff and tall with one casual arm leant on a steel tipped, jet-black cane. Even blacker boots anchored a slender frame. His face was the colour of the grit into which I buried mine, a rough and pale brown. A nose he couldn't help but look down. A top hat, and a frown.

Giant fragments of his voice broke off and bounced high around the tent. The drums rolled on, increasing their sickly pressure. They beat themselves to a silent apogee so stark in contrast to their beginnings that the crowd stood still and quiet and the lights lay down and shut their eyes. I drove my fingers into the gravel, which had grown warm beneath me, took a fistful in each palm and brought them together under my nose. It was so foreign. In the darkness I buried it back in its place and wept into the dirt.

One light opened up into a wink and pinched the master in its slightly sights. I was dragged from the tent by invisibles. I heard him say something like 'thank you, you've been a delight,' and something about 'two clowns to end the night.'

2

The next day the greatest show on earth rose. Shadows were cast long and opaque. Lamps flickered on and off down the aisle like the morning whispers of the waking. Smells were overwhelming – sweat and sex and sleep.

The master moved always with his assistant, Leopold, who would shuffle behind him with all the posture and personality of a hiding fugitive. His face was severely scarred, and his gait was bowed and crooked. He was a man of only quiet, hand wringing questions, and questions only to his master. That morning he searched the aisle for his only companion.

A pulse was pounding through the place, at first like gentle prints in sand, then like the low rolling of a drum. It was almost inaudible, and struck me from a sixth sense. Then the sun broke fully free above the trees and the world began to fade in and its sources became clearer: Slow footsteps slapping through waterlogged grass; rain on sheets of canvas; the tapping of a hammer on a tent peg; the padding of a black bear back and forth and back and forth in its cage; and a chopping coming from the porch of the master's caravan. Like a guillotine. Up, then down with a *chop*. Up, then down with a *chop*.

I woke up chained to a peg at the end of the aisle. I had spread myself out so that the drizzle caught the most of my skin. I lay with my head on my chin, watching the circus wake up. I felt that beat in time with the pulse in my head, I felt the pain of the whole place ebb in time with the ache in my temples, like the corridor was a river, and I a dam, and all of its agony crept towards me like driftwood. I saw myself in every morning face as people rose and began work.

'Sometime we are all in shackles,' I said aloud, then dipped my neck and rubbed my head back and forth in the dew.

The red and white striped tent had lost its inner glow. The big wheel lay still, as if broken, and time felt slow. The swell of excitement had melted away, replaced by the smell of bear shit. The music had vanished – not a single sign remained that it had ever existed – and was replaced by that pulsing, that *tap, tap, tap*, and that *chop, chop, chop*, patrolling the aisle.

The master was on the porch of his caravan, where his chopping added to that beat. He wore pinstripe trousers, a white shirt rolled up at the sleeves, and a blood-stained apron. The severed head of a bear sat in the seat of the chair beside him, its eyes dead but its teeth still grinning. The master chopped through the muscles and fat of the humbled animal.

When he was done he turned to the head and said, 'Now let's go and feed the animals.'

Later I met the bear tamer. He floated down the aisle like driftwood and caught himself in the silver dam of my chains. His cheeks were as moist as the morning with tears, his hair as grey as his beard.

I liked the bear tamer, he loved the bears like people sometimes love other people. He asked me if I believed in God. 'What is God?' I said.

'Where do you think we come from,' he asked, 'if not from some kind of God?'

'From the ground,' I said.

'That's not where we come from, but it is where we end up.'

I asked him what was wrong. 'Think about someone you care about as much as you could care about anything,' he said. 'Think about that feeling. Now think about how you would feel if that someone had an accident, killed in their line of work,' he said. I tried hard to think about that feeling. 'Now, how do you think you'd feel if that someone was cut into little pieces and fed to your friends and colleagues.'

I did not know.

'The circus has always been here or there or on its way. It's likely it always will be,' the tamer later told me. 'Frightening some with obscurity, and plucking others from it.

'They didn't call me the tamer before. The reckoning of my old name from the lips and minds of all these men began when I joined up here,' he said. 'I was who I was, I am who I am.'

'Who were you?' I asked.

'Nobody.

'As well the master has not always carried that weighty moniker.'

'Before?'

'Before he was a dentist. Way before. He sold his practice and bought this circus.'

The way the tamer talked made me uncomfortable in the early days, before I felt right just talking. He had a way of looking at me straight the whole time he spoke. Eyes looked out above a face never free from greying stubble, beneath thick eyebrows and a head of hair the wind was fond of styling in its own mad fashion. As he stared he breathed a slow and deep rhythm of breaths that made his chest swell and deflate visibly beneath his shirt and made the second of his chins move steady up and down.

At this time I didn't meet his gaze. Instead I dug around in the dirt with a stick, chiselling around a buried stone. I brushed the dust away gently with my fingers as if I were excavating something precious.

'What is a dentist?' I asked unlooking.

'A dentist is a man who fixes teeth. Sometimes a dentist hurts people, other times he hurts them in their pockets, but he always fixes them in the end. I have heard some stories about the how and why of the master changing from that particular line of work to this. Someone told me he heard that the master, working away way back on some yellow chompers, left the anaesthetic gas bottle flowing, filling his little workspace and his little brain. He fell and hit his head. After that, goes the story, he was never the same.'

'Do you believe it?'

'I don't believe it. I believe that when I first saw him he was a different man than he is now. The change has been a slight and slow one. We were old men then,' the tamer said to me, 'as we are now, but neither of us quite as broken.

With one levered movement of the stick I freed the submerged stone. It was a rugged thing that on one side was smooth and brown and eternal like an eye where it had once been a half of a large stone and had since become undone. It tumbled off across the ground with the force of its freedom. I smiled, pleased with myself, and looked up to share that smile with the tamer. I was met only with that same fixed stare.

'I was leaning back on his trailer, facing out across the dusty fields that bordered the little city I had spent two working decades in,' he said. 'There were a few sheep feeding on what was left of a grass that was yellower than it should have been in the glow of the sunset – or was it a sunrise? I was just thinking how nice it was, feeling how warm it was, and that I could get used to it. If work was what brought me there it didn't feel like it. I was a veterinarian, sick of the city, happy to be out of it. I leant back on his trailer, put my hand against my brow so as to shield my eyes from the sun and there he was. He hadn't been there moments ago, but there he was, sat on the fence right before me, as if he'd walked straight out of the sun and across the fields. He had his backside on the fence's top beam, and the heels of his boots hooked over the bottom. With one hand he held the wood, with the other he took a cigarette from between his lips and flicked its ash in the dirt. That same damned grin he wears now. He was twenty feet ahead of me, but when he spoke it was as if he whispered in my ear.

"You're here looking for work,' he said. 'What do you do?'

"I work with animals,' I said.

"Don't we all?"

When the tamer next saw the master he didn't. Instead he saw the cigarette smoke that masked him in his poorly lit trailer. Fake oak panels held the smell and yellow colour of a thousand more smoked. The light through blinds lay in stripes on those stained walls. The master reclined on a black leather dentist's chair. He exhaled as the tamer closed the door behind him, then swung his boots from the chair to the floor, thrust his face through the smoke that seeped from between his lips, hung briefly still in his wrinkles before drifting off wherever. Sat upright, the master smiled.

The corners of the room were not there, but blended with the night outside. It was likely the boy Leopold was somewhere where the panels shimmered black, but the tamer did not see him. Maybe a noise, a creak or tap carried somehow from that impossible vacuum that lay beyond the limits of the master's desk lamp and the bars of light that beat the blinds, but not a sight. The shriek of something caged beyond the edges of the edgeless trailer; inside just the smile of the master and the falling rising blue smoke around him.

'It'll be nice to have another educated man on staff,' he said. 'I take great pride in offering work to those who've struggled to find it, and normally I'd be reluctant to bring in a man with your career prospects. In this case I'll make an exception. I need an animal man. What, tell me, do you know about bears?'

'I've worked a little with farm animals,' said the tamer, 'but mostly domestic. Unfortunately bears are neither.'

'In some of the places I've visited they're both,' said the master. 'When I left the doctoral profession I knew nothing about the circus, about animals, about people beyond unimpressive incisors. I've learnt and I'm sure, with your qualifications, you'll learn too. A bear, for instance, has teeth not that dissimilar to a big dog's. You've worked with dogs?'

'Yes.'

'Big ones?'

'Sometimes.'

'Then you'll soon catch on with bears. We've got five meeting us next week. You say you like domestic animals? Well, it'll be your job to domesticate them.'

3

After a few more nights shackled in a dark patch, after a few more shows where I cowered and shook under the weight of entertainment, two clowns came to see me. They weaved their way through the aisle, a green bottle between them that they both held tight. Pockets with his left hand, and Tick with his right.

I had seen the clowns before, performing after me in the show. They rolled around the stage in clumsy ways, the crowded mouths that gaped at me laughing at them instead.

It was just after a show and their make-up had begun to fade. The smooth mask of comedy had been bent and creased by truth. It uncovered the tragedy of age and drink. The little light at my end of the aisle failed to penetrate the lines in their faces. Those dark lines revealed the clowns like maps.

Pockets wore a red waistcoat over a white shirt stained yellow in places with sweat from the heat of the stage lights. His trousers, spotty and baggy, seemed heavy with dirt and moist with the night. His shoes, one without a sole, were scuffed, brown and covered in mud, as if he had walked all the roads on the map of his face. Tick wore a smile where Pockets' face was marked sad. His trousers striped instead of spotted, and his waistcoat dirty blue.

I was awake, but had buried my face in the grass and breathed the heavy breath of sleep.

'I told you he'd be asleep,' whispered Tick, with a smile.

'Everyone's asleep,' replied Pockets, with a frown.

They circled me a little, passing the bottle between them, taking sips and wiping lips. They retained the rolling stumbles employed in their act, drunk, it seemed, both then and now.

'Besides,' said Pockets, 'how can you be so sure he's a he?'

Tick scratched his chin, ' I never said he was a he.'

'You said it just now. You *just* called him a he.'

'Well he clearly is, just look at his hair,' said Tick. 'It's short, like a he.'

'Good point. I think he must be,' concluded Pockets, passing the bottle back to his partner.

'What's his name?' asked Tick, 'Tell me and I'll wake him.'

'Caliban.'

'What kind of a name is that?'

'It's *his* name.'

Tick leaned towards me until I could smell a new thing; the liquor on his breath. 'Caliban,' he said softly, 'wake up.'

'Is he your sweetheart?' said Pockets. 'Don't make love to him, *wake him.*'

'What do you suggest I do?'

'Give him a poke.'

'I thought you didn't want me to make love to him?' They sniggered and sipped at the bottle. 'Do you think he bites?'

'No.'

'Are you sure?'

'No.'

Tick stepped forward until he was consumed in the dark patch. 'Oh God,' he said, 'he smells awful.'

'I think that's the bear intestines.'

'I don't think he's got bear intestines, Pockets. How would I even smell them through all that skin and scales?'

Pockets gestured at a pile of meat that sat nearby. A gift from the master, who had gotten upset when I refused to eat it. I do not eat a friend of my friend the tamer. 'How peculiar,' the master had said, inspecting my teeth. 'He's biologically determined to eat meat – just look at his teeth – yet he refuses.'

After the clowns woke me they took me to their trailer, a dilapidated thing with a bent poled, canvas porch outside protecting two deckchairs and a small fire from the rain. Its roof sagged in the middle with water collected from that two day drizzle; a reflected moon fractured and broken by the equable raindrops that beat it into a melody of shifting, yellow shapes.

The front of the porch was poorly tied up in a roll, from which water dripped and pooled with a slap in the mud.

Pockets and Tick were always talking. But talking to *me*. I became a whore with chatter. I listened and felt warmer – although perhaps that was the fire. Or perhaps the thick liquor in that green bottle.

At first I had refused a drink, put off by the smell of it, but soon I found putting that liquid inside me as natural as releasing it from the other end.

'Are you sure you won't have a drink?' Pockets had said. 'Fair enough, it's best you stay off it, really. Tick and I are quite taken with it.'

'Stricken by it,' said Tick.

'So you've probably made the right choice there, Caliban.'

'Or the wrong choice.'

'Around here, probably the wrong choice.'

Whilst the clowns drank, I asked what I was and why I was there.

'You're a slave,' said Pockets.

'No,' said Tick, 'slaves don't get paid.'

'I don't think he's getting paid.'

'What is paid?' I asked.

'It doesn't matter, since you're not getting it.'

'But it's not all that bad,' said Pockets. 'You can have a drink with us. Why, that's practically getting paid, seeing as how you're not paying for it.'

So I drank for the first time and it was good. We sank deep into the murky-blue night, and deeper into a slow and stumbled three man debauch. Eventually, as the sun got its yellow fingers over the shelf of the horizon, our chatter drifted onto the master, the king of our aisle. The clowns explained to me a new thing; he was our employer, our ringmaster.

The sun got a full arm over the Earth and pushed its fingers through the trees, spilling light across the roofs of trailers and tents, bouncing from dew drop to dew drop and turning everything into crystal dawn. The world span around me, along with the clowns, and time passed without so much as a footprint of memory. Except I remember them dance.

Pockets stood in front of us and made the porch a stage. He lost his balance, regained it, and cleared his throat. 'Gentlewomen and ladies, can I have your attention please,' he said, swinging about the porch, throwing his arms in exaggerated gestures of showmanship. 'My name is the master, king of the jungle – or something – and I've got some stuff for you tonight. *Have I got some special stuff for you tonight?* I've got tigers from Tigeria, bears from Bearasia, lions from Liontarctica, and elephants from – somewhere. All in this tent. All for you.'

He sniggered, and I took the bottle from him.

'Give that back or I won't introduce you,' he said. I took a sip and handed it back, grinning in the company of my friends.

'Introduce me now,' I said.

'After the clowns,' he said, 'because we've got clowns as well. The best clowns this side of...'

'Anywhere,' said Tick.

'*Anywhere*. They're the best clowns this side of anywhere. After them we have a real treat for you, a real feast for your senses: *Caliban*.'

I took the clowns by their hands and we jumped and danced around the dying fire.

'*'Ban, 'Ban, Ca-Caliban*,' sang Pockets, passing me the bottle. 'He's got a new master, now get a new man.'

'*'Ban, 'Ban, Ca-Caliban*,' the three of us chanted together. 'Drinks wine from the bottle in a caravan.'

Then a chair was kicked over. It landed on the fire's last embers, putting them out, and we were left with only the sobering light of dawn.

'Shut those fucking clowns up,' someone shouted from somewhere.

4

Soon after my first meeting with the clowns the circus packed up and left whatever town we were in. I never learnt its name.

Another new thing: We left the town in trucks and caravans and I watched the things pass by like flying photographs; snapshots of buildings and countryside and all the people. All of the people that I'd never seen before. I had learnt about talking, and a little about friends, and I was so curious to speak to them, but I wondered why the master would cage us, hide us away from them, if not to protect us. I shied away from the windows, but kept on peeking, both afraid and yearning for what flew by outside. We left the outside people trailing behind us like long scarves in the wind.

On the first trip I travelled by myself, cramped in a caravan amongst bags of potatoes, stacks of fliers and boxes of tricks. After a few journeys, a few new towns and cities, I was no longer so lonely. I learnt the ways of our ever floating aisle, and was allowed a morsel of freedom. I learnt about a thing called a vice, and how everyone at the circus was trapped inside their own, unable to leave the aisle.

My vice was my appearance. The master told me that outside of the aisle the people found me hideous – hence my value to the show. Inside the aisle my colleagues did not notice this vice, so occupied they were with not being suffocated by their own. The clowns, for example, were rotten with drink, the tamer drowning in a thickening depression.

I was given the freedom of the aisle as a reward for doing my job. I growled around a pit for twenty minutes a night, and was in turn allowed to live without chains, to do as I pleased and to make a modest bed for myself under the canvas porch of Pockets and Tick's trailer. I was no longer marched into the ring by the point of a knife, and discovered that weapons and trust were often interchangeable.

Despite this morsel of freedom, I dared not stray further than the invisible limits of our shanty town, warned by others of the cruelty that lay in wait in the darkness beyond. I wondered, but I did not wander.

After a time another bear died. The small family, it seemed, had become unsettled and had turned to murder. I thought how people and animals could be so alike. I thought about God, whom the tamer had told me of, and I thought about where the bears might be now that they were gone. If, as I'd been told, but was yet to believe, there was life after death, then did people share it with animals, as they share almost everything else?

One night I had a dream that every bug I had squashed and killed under my feet came back as ghosts to haunt me. They crawled around invisible, following me everywhere. When I was still they covered me and bit at my flesh, unbeknownst to me, until I was under a sheet of writhing revenge. They made a black crown on my head, my face the unsuspecting jewel of accidental power, and waited for me to pass over, when I would finally atone for my genocide.

When I woke up there was a spider on my chest. I cupped him in my hands and placed him outside the porch in the grass, away from my clumsy omnipotence.

Another I was asleep and another pair approached me. Two young girls who worked the hall of mirrors, picked up in a previous town and bound to leave at the next. Again I was awake, and again I breathed heavy and fake.

'He is terrible,' said one.

'Truly,' said the other.

'I knew this place was *fucked*, but he's got to be the worst. Look at his skin.'

'It's like scales.'

'Have you seen his eyes? I swear, they're dead inside.'

'He's a monster.'

A common thing: I peeked between my fingers. One was close. The other peered over her shoulder. They looked here but somehow not at me. The closer was tall and blonde and pretty even though she scowled.

'Did he just move?' she said.

'Let's get out of here,' said the other and they did.

One time we set our travelling show on a beach, and I saw two things fully for the first time. I saw the sea, and I saw myself reflected in it.

It was my first spring with the circus, the winter still battling with the summer in the early and late parts of the day. In the afternoon I walked on the beach where we had pitched our tents and trailers and took in the sea as smooth as glass. The sea and the sky are not always so calm, they are often very passionate, I have learnt, always arguing and making a fuss over nothing.

I saw myself in the shallows. I was not amazed. The face staring back at me was not unlike the one my fingers had whispered to my mind. The skin on my face was as stretched and coarse as on the rest of my body, the hair on my head as thick and black as that of my chest and back. My eyes were the most interesting. They were green. I thought maybe I had looked too long at the trees and the grass around the fields we had sometimes camped in and they had turned my eyes green. I thought that if I stayed on the beach and starred at the sea they would turn blue, or if I closed them for days they would turn black.

5

Once in the late day the horizon, on the other side than the sea, seemed a monochrome stencil. Its features pencilled words, black against a moon mostly set. The sky paper-white except for a jagged language printed upon it in the black shapes of trees or the occasional rooftop parentheses. Sometimes the silver smudge of a cloud.

Between the illegible horizon and I were fields and fields and fields. They were a thick, deceptive lens, the rain streaked window through which I strained at some foreign sign. All that told me those distant lines were not the very end of a story, miles and miles and miles away, was the reassuring perspective of a deer fence between two of the fields. Its posts and wires were hidden here and there with the bony hands of trees stripped of their leaves by the open country's wind. All threw long shadows across the fields. Another deer fence, twice my height at least, separated us from the fields and the horizon's scrawled lines.

Sounds, heartless, heatless, and unreadable and fields and fields and fields away. They were as black and white and grey as the distance they came from. There was a sharp bark, a short wait, then a barrage of them in a quick and penetrating sequence that sent birds from

trees in heavy clumps. I was glad at least two tall fences
separated the circus and the barking in the distance.

I watched the birds that moved about an otherwise
empty sky in a fluid unity. They were a dark and dancing
cloth, torn to a wretched net, beautiful and devastatingly
fragmented. The cloud of birds moved to another tree in
another field, and laid its soft instrument down in the
tree's bare branches. They are only to move again,
I thought, at the next scare, always the same pretty
patterns in the sky, the same imperfect design. Lesson
missed from tree to tree to tree.

In the aisle people moved less in harmony, but still in
a recognisable and predictable pattern in which I was
beginning to grow comfortable.

After the birds had roosted I was shifting through the
straw floor upon which sat the tent, the bleachers, the
crowd's roar; softened its joining with the earth, a dead,
brown, laid down bulwark of itching, yellow thatch.
I scratched around in it and must have appeared to be
looking for something. I was staying out of the way,
waiting for the clowns. Sometimes I would hide out
there, where the lamps from the ring got between the
bleachers in thin strips and covered the straw beneath
in sideways yellow bars of light. I'd peak out between
the wooden benches, between the black leather shoes
of men and the slighter, tiny strapped slippers of
their partners. I'd watch the show without concern,
and scratch around in the straw with my bare feet,
enjoying the itching, biting sensation on my soles and
between my toes.

A body came through the shadows as the crowd
applauded the clowns from the ring. A short thing –
almost as low as me amongst the beams and rafters that

held up the bleachers. Less awkward in its movements, not especially, but with limbs obliging each other as it ducked beams and stepped over mounds of straw. I saw a blouse; open a little beneath the neck, breasts, short legs that dragged dust up from the straw as they disturbed it with squat and firm strides. Light came through the seats in slanted streaks. Though those stripes worked across me like bars on a cage, she played them like the blocks of a marimba. They danced across her in harmonies.

When she was closer I saw that there was nothing special about the way she moved. She was not, it seemed, some fantastic creature blown in here by mistake with the leaves, a dust dervish, caught and spiralling like my mind had told my eyes a beautiful girl would be. Her limbs were quick and graceless as they formed words in shapes in a small space in front of her breast. Behind them her chest rose and fell slightly beneath a silk white shirt and her neck sat on it almost clumsily, jogged her head as she spoke through her hands.

Her face was flat – not as flat as mine – almost unreadable, so far removed was language from her mouth that it barely moved at all, lips perhaps a little limp, mouth a little open. If it did move it was without sound and without meaning. All that was in her hands.

It did not take me long to figure out that she could not speak and could not hear. I had seen her earlier amongst the crowd, small and almost hidden like something precious and desperate to be found. She didn't seem to understand what was going on at all. Didn't jump at cannon bursts, didn't react to the clowns' or the master's jokes or taunts. She sat apart from the rest, who melded into a dark blur.

'Hello,' I said simply beneath the bleachers. She shook her head and moved her hands with a practiced precision. They wound about themselves in artisanal bursts, saying something I couldn't understand. She signed and stopped, her little jaw dropped, upon realising there was no way past the insurmountable semantic wall between us.

Her hair lay only as far as her chin, and curled around her round face in a honey coloured frame. It bounced when she moved her head, as if on springs from her scalp, and its tips tickled the top of her neck. She tried again the thing with her hands.

'I'm sorry that I don't know what you're doing,' I said. 'It looks very nice.'

She shrugged and took my hands, went I think to kiss my cheek but stopped when stopping was almost impossible. I felt her breath touch my cheek, released and made contact like the least finger and I shivered.

She moved her lips and nothing came out but breath. I turned and watched her mouth wordless holes. *You were*, she mimed, *created in a star*. She touched my cheek, withdrew her hand and looked at her fingertips, expected to see I don't know what. Ashes. Blood. To see them wrinkled with time or cracked like mine. She touched my cheek again but this time kept her hand there. Time wrinkled. I shivered and pulled back, looked at her and saw she had a tear in her eye. She mouthed something I could not understand, tried to sign.

'What?' I said, but I am not sure I made a sound. It did not matter if I did. She turned around and through the bars of light she left.

I watched a little while through the bleachers. The show was ending with a band and feet struck their wooden rests along to the rhythm. Men in red coats blew into coiled brass instruments of different sizes, one wrapped around a man like a golden snake, another as small as the fore of my arm. I tried to watch without listening, as I thought the girl would be, but couldn't. I thought how strange it would be to not hear. How strange those men would seem without the music vamping and the crowd's feet tapping. I put my hands over my ears and tried again. I could not completely shut out the music, trap it in the air before it entered my ear, as it sought to move from host to host, but the underwater babel that this made still gave the red coated men the noise they needed to exist without confusion, and with my hands pushing and my eyes straining I saw her again.

She retook her seat and watched the band as I had tried to – deafened.

6

'What do you think makes us men?' asked Pockets that night. 'How much wine we drink? How many times we have peeled the dress from a woman like a banana skin, and split her legs like its fruit? Or how many times we've filled these blankets with tears and left it wet in the morning for work?'

He grinned a little, one that turned south at the corners. He looked at us both and sipped red wine from a bottle. When he brought it from his lips they were stained red. His teeth, too, were darker.

'I hope it's not the second one,' I said.

'Which one was that?' said Tick.

'I was being rhetorical,' said Pockets.

'Even so, which one was that?'

'The one about the girl.'

'Why do you hope it wasn't the one about the girl?'

'Because that experience is unusual to me, and I would like to be a man.'

'I'm sure it's not the one about the girl, and I'm sure you are a man,' said Tick.

'The answer is the last one,' said Pockets. 'The grindstone. The one that shouldn't be unusual to any of us three. I reckon what makes us men is our ability to endure the unendurable.'

We felt the presence, maybe for the first time, of a far off urgency that night. It played around us like children in a park. We were only partially aware. Occasionally it would stumble and fall right in front of us, and we would consider it silently, but for the most part it fluttered unnoticed in the periphery.

The night sky was so much clearer by the sea. The stars were beautiful, as if someone had pulled a sheet across the sun, pricked little holes in it, and the sun was peeking through watching the world in secret.

That night I dreamed I carved a boat from a tree, and cast off from the beach, just my reflection and me.

7

The master left the circus by the beach for a few days, as he did from time to time. He left us in the charge of Leopold. The week was not uneventful, though, I met a new but altogether familiar man.

The salesman's carriage was the oldest thing I'd ever seen. Pulled by a sorry looking horse, it rolled into our aisle like something I'd only heard about in stories. It emerged from the mist and into our lives as if through time travel; the slow clip-clop of hooves, and the click-clack of two wooden wheels, ticking by their revolutions with all the slow, metronomic grace of giant clocks.

The salesman, too, was thrown towards us from a different time. He dressed not dissimilarly to the master, although he was more rotund and had a perfect, pencil-thin moustache. He wore a top hat, the brim and his thick eyebrows meeting in the middle of a small forehead. The buttons of his shirt were pulled to breaking point across his midriff, but he appeared generally clean, if a little out of sorts. He drove the horse from a small seat at the front of his covered carriage. One gloved hand held the reigns, the other his hat against the wind.

The side of the carriage read 'Ike Wright's Trailer of Light' in ornate, gold lettering. There was a painting of the salesman, Ike Wright, on the side too, smiling and looking thinner.

It was in the early hours of the morning, not a show day, that Ike arrived. Most observed him roll up with a lazy curiosity. Without moving from their porches and deckchairs they inspected him over steaming coffee cups. An unsolicited intruder into the aisle was usually ignored until he left, or sent back the way he came quickly enough. In that way our world was not unlike the wider.

Ike dismounted and tied his horse off to an old fence post. The horse pulled a little, but had neither the strength or will to break the already crumbling wood. He watched after Ike as he moved into the aisle, and eventually went to lapping water from a muddy puddle. I felt sorry for the horse. His coat was grey with age rather than nature, and his ribcage was as bare and weak as the row of fence posts he was tied to. I thought that this salesman might be leaving on foot if he didn't find a new horse soon.

I listened to him talk from a distance. Like the master he was a sculptor of words. Those he spoke to regarded him with suspicion as he approached, but after a few minutes had unfolded their arms and beamed at him with new friendship. A few minutes more and they were shaking hands and offering him a drink, despite the early hour. I noticed that he never drank, only clicked his cup with theirs and took a tiny sip – maybe didn't even let a drop past his lips.

'I know how you must feel, fella,' he said as he came upon Leopold, the master's assistant. 'Moving around all the time really takes it out of me. Old Beeswax, too,' he gestured at the grey horse.

'He doesn't look like he's got anything left to take out,' said Leopold in his deep and quite voice. He did not look up from his breakfast.

'That horse is sixty years old, and I bet he's pulled my carriage for more miles this week than this circus has moved in a month. He's the greatest horse that ever lived.'

Leopold allowed himself a look at Beeswax, 'A horse for a course,' he said. 'We use motors here. If he's that old he's an impressive animal, but he'll never outlive or outrun a train.'

'You're a smart man. You know why I came straight over to you? I've got an eye for spotting the bosses, the decision makers. I bet you're one of the top men here. No, wait, *the* top man here.'

Leopold smiled and adjusted his hair with his left hand. With his right he put down his breakfast. He moved his feet from an adjacent stool, allowing the salesman to join him. 'Would you like a coffee, Mr Wright?' he said.

'Call me Ike.'

I went to say hello to Beeswax the horse. Whilst I did Ike sold Leopold one thousand bottles of a drink called Luminous Vigour, a yellow potion that had supposedly doubled Beeswax's strength, speed, and lifespan. I listened to their conversation from my position by the horse with little interest.

'Hello, Beeswax,' I said. He gave me a long and sorry look, regarded me with no enthusiasm or emotion, and stood droopily still, only tiny movements like that of glass. I stroked his forehead and his ears. I saw he must have gotten his name from the colour of his coat, before he had turned old and grey. There were still some honey hued hairs here and there. I looked for them over his body, stroking him as I went. He began to wheeze, and then returned to being motionless, which seemed his favourite way to be. Has such prolonged human contact made you so lifeless and empty, I thought. Maybe you are just waiting to die.

Ike had finished his business with Leopold, and was moving further down the aisle when he was interrupted by another man, a stagehand from the circus.

'Did I hear you say that horse was *sixty* years old?' he said.

'Yes you did. You're a very observant chap,' said Ike. 'Let's sit down and I'll tell you all about it.'

I stayed with Beeswax a little longer, but started to grow tired of his unmoving self-pity. I could not, no matter how hard I tried, illicit any emotional response from him. I tickled his nose and he sneezed a cold, black snot into my hands. That was as friendly as we became.

The label on those bottles read:

Ike Wright's Luminous Vigour, it's everything you want in a bottle.

It revives and sustains, brightens moods and relieves pains.

It'll keep away your nightmares and curlify your chest hairs.

It's life prolonging, wind escaping, erection giving, ambrosia, eternal sunshine in a bottle.

Extend your endurance, gain new assurance.

We've got extra bottle out the bottle, no more wobble in your throttle.

If you can't endure it, let us cure it with Ike Wright's Luminous Vigour.

For the next few days everyone was drinking it, including myself. Leopold had distributed bottles around, saying something about it becoming our endorsed drink, and selling them at the shows. I wondered how the master would feel about this.

It wasn't a bad tasting potion, like fizzy but not unpleasant chemicals. If it did what it promised on the label then it was a very special drink indeed. I didn't like the thought, however, of putting something so unnatural inside me. The bubbles burned my throat a little, and I thought it would do the same to my insides. Its slight glow was also a little unsettling.

The arrival of Ike Wright and his mysterious potions lifted the mood around the aisle. His drink brought promises that seemed to be fulfilled, as people's virility increased and they found the energy to talk and socialise.

Ike himself seemed content to stay awhile. As an individual's supply of Luminous Vigour disappeared he went to that old carriage to get some more, adding them to the bill.

In the evenings Ike would chat and pretend to drink with Leopold, and the two seemed to thrash out great, joint plans. One morning I saw that scarred and miserable man smiling, washing Ike's shirt in a tin tub. He hung it carefully outside the salesman's carriage and waited patiently for his new friend to wake up.

It was on Ike Wright's third day in the aisle that I spoke with him. I was the only circus worker not to have visited him personally to procure more Vigour. In fact, when he approached me I was sipping and grimacing at the mostly full bottle given to me two days before.

'You don't look like you're enjoying that, son?' Ike said. He dropped to one knee, brought his face in line with mine, and took off his top hat.

'It's a strange potion,' I said. 'It's not unlikable, but I think not for me.'

'Come on, son,' he said with a smile, 'all of your friends are drinking it.'

'I'm sure you've noticed I am a little different from the most of them.'

He looked around the aisle, his eyes briefly following one, then another, then another of the aisle's more conventionally human employees. He took his time to compare them and me.

'Now you mention it,' he said, 'there are a few small differences.'

'I am surprised you did not notice straight away.'

'They're not so bad, those little differences,' he said. 'But they must be hard on you. The little things are accentuated in one's own eyes.'

'Accentuated?'

'You take that hall of mirrors over there, manned by that darling blonde.'

'She is beautiful.'

'I love these fairground frivolities, but if there's one thing I don't like it's the mirrors in those places. There's one that seems to bulge in the middle. I remember standing in front of one that blew my belly up like a balloon. I'm a portly man, and always notice so. That mirror made me look even bigger, *accentuated* my gut,' he slapped his protruding stomach. 'It made me feel different.'

'Really?'

'I trimmed the fat from my meat for a week.'

I heard somewhere that atoms, which are incomprehensibly tiny pieces of things, spend their time both repelling and attracting each other. In that way, a person is always trying desperately to both implode and explode. We are made of destructive things. The salesman was no different. In fact, these atomic characteristics were more evident in him than most anyone. Altogether he was cocooned in isolated thought, turned in on himself and working deep in there at break neck speed. At the same time he was always ready to burst, unable to contain the overflowing machinations of his internal brilliance.

Ike Wright promised me a cure. He said he had a potion in his carriage that could grow me, unbow me, smooth my skin, and make me much the same as everyone else. I found this a troubling idea. My abnormalities provided me with a place to live and a purpose for myself. A use for a person should never be underestimated. I was not sure that I was happy, but I was sure that I was *useful*, and was wary of removing the only thing that I had. I wondered if there was happiness to be found inside the crowd.

I was thinking all of these things when Ike Wright said 'See that girl who works the hall of mirrors? If you were a normal looking man I bet you could meet a nice girl like her.'

I agreed to try his cure.

I wouldn't have to pay straight away. He explained that I should try it and see how it turned out before buying a whole lot. As I drank the miracle cure, a thick, brown ooze, I wondered what he meant.

The spritely atmosphere around the aisle continued in parallel to the people's consumption of Luminous Vigour. I refused the glowing stuff, much to the scorn of Ike and Leopold, but forced bottle after bottle of that new, brown silt into my body. Ike brought me a new one every morning, careful to chat a little, ask how I was, but surprisingly ignored the subject of my abnormalities and the elixir's promised effects until his seventh day with us.

By this time Ike was completely at home on the aisle. He had always moved about it with confidence, but now with added respect. People asked his opinion on life's mundanities, and he gave it to them willingly, often with a bottled or ground remedy tagged on. Luminous Vigour had lasted the week and was growing in popularity. The clowns even used it to dilute their harsher spirits.

On that seventh day he meandered down the aisle along with Leopold, stomach pushed out in front of him and his head swinging from side to side, offering a 'hello' to his left and a 'good day' to his right.

'My God,' he said when he came to me. 'I think it's starting to work.' He looked me up and down, held his hand above my head as if to judge my height, and took on a look of deep concentration, all of his atoms trying to implode and explode him.

'*Yes*!' he said. 'It's starting to work. I'd say you were at least two inches taller. Perhaps more. Your skin looks softer, too. How *remarkable*. I knew it would work, but I didn't expect results quite so quickly. What do you think?' he asked Leopold, who hadn't really been watching.

'I think so, Ike,' he said after a pause.

'Well there you go, that settles it. It works like a charm. What do you say, Caliban? I'd like to offer you a bulk discount. I think a bottle a day for the next couple of months will turn you into a man. About a hundred notes should cover it all.'

It was hard not to like this man when everybody else loved him so. To trust him was to take a step towards normality, to drink that brown potion an apparently big jump. At that moment I wanted to continue with his treatment, but did not have the money, and was anyway a little unsure of the formalities of its exchange.

'I do not have that money,' I said.

'It's a lot, I admit. You should pay your staff better,' he said to Leopold. 'They do a fine job and should be able to afford such a revolutionary product. '

Leopold went to speak, raised an indignant finger, but Ike cut him off. 'How about ninety,' he said. 'I'll be staying here for a little while. You can even pay me in instalments.'

'I still cannot afford it.'

'My God,' he said, throwing up his arms and turning to Leopold. 'This poor fellow is trying to sort himself out, and you can't give him ninety measly notes to improve his wretched quality of life? This is why I got into medicine, Caliban, to help poor souls like yours.'

'What I think he means,' said Leopold, 'is that he doesn't have any money at all. He is owned by the circus. We don't pay him anything.'

Ike's face turned a dark and stormy shade of red, then turned to me. 'You mean,' he said, 'that these past few days you've been taking my product knowing full well that you neither had, nor ever would have, any reasonable means of payment?'

I backed away. Ike's breath grew heavy as his atoms pushed him to explode. His face creased up like balled paper, bringing all of his features together into an indistinguishable mess below his shallow, frowning forehead.

'You mean that you have been *stealing* from a reputable businessman,' he said, and spun towards Leopold, bringing with him a louder voice. 'And *you* let this happen.'

Ike's expression returned to normal in an instant, his face flattened out and his voice turned immediately softer. He pulled on his shirt cuffs, composed himself.

'Well, I hold you and the circus entirely culpable for the full value, one hundred notes, of the stock this creature has stolen. Furthermore, I expect you to pay me the rest of the money owed for the Luminous Vigour immediately. It's the only way we can put this ugliness behind us and carry on doing business civilly. Doing business as friends.'

'Of course, Ike. I'm so sorry,' said Leopold. 'I want to be friends.' The salesman put his arm around him, as if the two were old companions, and began to lead him away.

The master returned two days later to find Ike Wright firmly in charge of the aisle and with a large amount of the circus' money in his carriage. Ike recognised the master. He pleaded and apologised, claiming he didn't know whose circus it was, and that he would return some of the money. They could strike a deal, he suggested. The master brought him by the ear through the aisle, paraded him to his subjects as a false shepherd, sculpted words and insults that broke Ike into pieces. We saw him for who he was then. If there ever was a man to rival the master the inhabitants of the aisle thought they had found him in Ike Wright, but the master showed them otherwise. Ike was a trickster and a thief, and was called much worse as he crawled to his carriage.

'I do not *deal* with fucks like you,' said the master.

Beeswax the horse defied mortality once more. I would never have thought that horse could move quickly, but Ike whipped it and yelled at it and smacked its hind quarters and Beeswax, at a fast trot, dragged that sorry carriage back into the mist and out of our lives forever.

'You ugly lapdog,' the master said to Leopold as the hunched and broken man followed him to his trailer. 'You have always been a coward, always brought me nothing but trouble. If I should have kicked you out of here to die before I sure as hell should now.'

I chastised myself in private for drinking that potion. I was angry at myself for believing what Ike Wright had said to me, for allowing him to lead me blindly down his path while closing off all others. In doing so I'd facilitated his brand of cruelty and let it spread a little in world. The desire to be identical was as normal to humans as he made me want to be, and perhaps the most damning thing our pushing, pulling atoms made us do. We were all different people, our only commonality being looked upon by the masters and the salesman of the world as the same. To look around the aisle was to see a people so diverse as to appear a hundred different species. And that, I thought, was a good thing.

8

People like to see remarkable children. That was how it was with Leopold long before I arrived at the circus. The world's strongest boy to a broken man. The tamer told me how Leopold was there when he arrived, not four feet high but able to lift three times what any man could.

'There was and still is no doubt in my mind that he was not a natural child,' the tamer said to me. 'A surprise would be if the master hadn't made some potion to change his very DNA in that lab of a trailer he hides in. I'll be damned if I'm the one to ask him so, though.'

The tamer told me how Leopold was once just a boy. He had a barrel for a chest and wine bottles for arms, but he was just a boy. Often unseen, unheard, he was a rare thing – independent from a master who adored him. He spent long summer days reading the books the master bought him with.

'We would talk sometimes,' said the tamer, 'as likeminded people do, much like we are now, except he was a more learned conversationalist. Where you ask questions, he'd try and answer them, but they were his all the same. The curiosity of the young; it will likely be your undoing.'

'Was it his?'

'Of course.'

'What would you talk about?'

'What he was reading, usually, and he'd tie himself in knots trying to fill the holes those books had opened up for him. Science was of interest, and we'd discuss the biology of my animals. He spoke entirely then in questions and answers. 'What is a bear,' he'd ask, 'if it's neither a big cat nor a big dog?' Then, rambling, he'd answer it himself before I could say a word. Incidentally the bear is more like a dog than a cat, its closest living relatives include the wolf and, you might find surprising, the seal. I learnt that from Leopold.

'Religion was a subject he was more interested in. It let his answers amble, find not a conclusion but more of the questions that he loved to ask. He was fascinated with the bible and its contradictions. He'd try endlessly to solve them like a puzzle. If he'd wanted to, though, he could have torn that book in two.

'As did the crowd, the master put him upon an unassailable pedestal. People like to see remarkable children. You might think otherwise, but little things scare them more than big things.'

'Like me?'

'That is why they like you. Their reaction is why the master loved him, and I suspect why that affection has transcended Leopold's descent into adulthood. The master is not a man to find a use for just anyone.

'He had the body of a strongman five times his age but the face of a boy, of pure light. He pulled in crowds with both, and that was why the master loved him.'

The tamer told me about Leopold's shows. 'They left a hole,' he said. Sometimes they'd involve staged fights with large men where the boy would lift them above his head, drop them to the ground, and bay and flex in the dust cloud. The master's eyes, he didn't study his audience, but kept them on Leopold.

9

I rose one morning before the rest as the wind was icy cold and tossed the sea about the shore, spray coming up the beach and painting the sand a mottled canvas of yellows and dark browns between the shadows of the clouds and everything freckled by rain and blown over itself by the wind. The sky was grey and low and there were no lights save the sun behind the clouds that somehow still lit the world. I went to the shore and stood with the water at my toes, where every few seconds the furthest reach of waves would stretch and stretch and then recede. The sea and the calls of its birds were all the sounds there were and they were not unpleasant to me.

I went further into the water and tried to see myself again in it. It was either too dark or the water too rough. I hunched and could not see my face, could not see the bottom of the shallows, only the darkness of my frame dancing over waves where I blocked the sun's little light and no heat from the patch of ocean I observed. I walked out a little further until the water came up to my stomach. There it lifted me off my feet and I floated cold but unafraid about the growing surf. I lay on my back and watched a bird carry something wriggling overhead. The sea broke about me softly.

Quickly I was on top of it then altogether under it with one rolling hand of a wave that brushed me beneath its fingers, tickling swell and spray and to the shifting silt that lay black at its floor dark and infinite like the slick skin of some always sleeping lizard, pebbles and shells and eyes and claws. I got a toe to the floor and an eye upwards and found I was at a depth beyond my height. Then I was under another wave. On the bottom a white shell or the very top of something's skull, scalped and separated and lying bleached by the sun from its time on the beach and weathered smooth by waves and just the dome showing like beneath the sand a man stood to attention altogether white and yellow and skeletal. I pushed away from the seabed's penumbra but another wave was equal to my efforts and I curled and tumbled embryonic about the undercurrent. Before me bubbles streamed from between my lips without my asking and their rushing to the surface was the only way I knew which way was up. They grew and warped and moved into a brighter patch where some shape swam otherworldly in the twinkling broken surface and I breathed in to replace them and choked and spat and drowned.

There was a sickly black weed, thick and rooted deeper than a whale's dive and colder and more still than the lifeless body of one aged and sunken and dead. Then there were two of them. As my lungs filled more with water I grasped the trunks and uprooted them but they kicked me away and I saw that they were boots. I was turned upside down by something above me. I grabbed again at the weeds and was sure that they were a pair of boots. I was lifted up and let them slip from my grip as my mind turned black as their wet leather.

The tamer swears the master held me by my ankle between his thumb and his forefinger, slapped me with a naked palm, its glove held in his other, until I coughed and awoke hanged there. He plucked me from the sea as if I were a thing of curiosity found whilst ambling along the beach. I came up hair dripping and coughing water from my lungs. It escaped from me in falling columns and returning to the sea as quickly as it could. He watched me silently. I waved my arms and tried to grab something. The sun had broken through the clouds and in the yellow morning had already begun to dry me as I hung there in the master's hand. The ocean that had seemed so deep and impossible only rising as far as the tops of his legs and no higher than his waist when the waves broke around him like those that broke on great rocks or cliffs.

I wriggled coughing, a worm on a hook, got a look at the master with his back to the sun and the shore behind him a pastel thing and the sky alight in red and orange and blue and white. Birds pecked through the circus' debris on the beach, great white things with our scraps in their beaks and the sun on their wings. In my baptismal robes of sodden hair and rags I dripped upended in the master's hand. With two of his strides we were on the sands and the birds scattered down the beach with their wings outstretched and some took off and circled the beach before landing further down the shore.

The master placed me in the sands and I lay rasping, lungs rattling, water seeping from the corner of my mouth. The master picked his hat from the sand and placed it on his head then took off up the beach towards the tents and huts where people had begun to gather and fix their breakfast. Some that had watched my toiling and my saving from the safety of the camp turned and went about their business. I lay on my back and that new morning sun that had arrived at my submersion dried me out. Sand crusted in my hair and I shook it out as I soon rose and followed the master's heavy tracks up the shore and into camp.

10

The growing rumble of an impending show spread itself out across the beach, our noise replacing the easy hush of waves. As the sun sank into the ocean our lights came on and lit the racket into clear purpose. The big wheel started up into slow action, and the red and white striped tent began to glow from within. People trickled in and out of it carrying signs, chairs, costumes, and boxes of props.

I sat in the sand and watched it all. I saw Pockets and Tick swigging from a bottle by their trailer. I saw them practice a little. They juggled, danced, cartwheeled and pranced, but mostly passed the bottle back and forth.

I saw Leopold frantically pace about, consulting everyone and everything in wheezing heavy, spitting breaths. He'd stop and stand still, make a note on a clipboard. Then he'd be off and moving again, zigzagging along the beach between caravans and cages, men and animals. Eventually he disappeared into the master's trailer and didn't return until both men came out together. The master moved with long, deliberate strides. Leopold skipped and limped alongside, relaying information from his clipboard to his boss. The master stretched a black glove between his hands, put it on, then did the same with another. He used his cane to point at this and that as he moved through the aisle, his directions transferred from his assistant to the clipboard.

Eventually the two disappeared into the tent, beyond which a buzzing had begun to rise. A queuing, impatient crowd tussled amongst themselves. They waited in the bitter sea wind for the red and white curtain to open and the show to start.

I had grown prone to getting caught up in the excitement before a show. I had made some friends about the aisle, and had learnt my place and trade. We were all fed by the same hand, and had all thought of biting it, but the time had never been right.

Something had grown hungry.

Shortly after the lights of the circus were switched on the last waning crescent of the sun joined the rest at the bottom of the sea. It left fractured beams for just a second, scattered across the waves and the sunken bellies of low clouds. Afterwards the orange glow of the town monopolised the sky. Music started out of nowhere and echoed around the aisle so that it reached me sounding like a round. The crowd had entered the tent and their chattering caused it to bulge and quiver. I made my way inside.

This time I entered the ring at my own choosing. The crowd still bayed and booed however, as I made my way to its centre. As my eyes adjusted I began to make out the silhouettes of faces. Those hollow faces. The rest was a murky obscure, as if the whole audience were dressed in black. Their jeers too, fused into one tyrannical howl which never failed to shake me to my bones.

This time I bayed back. I made the ring mine with anger and hate on all fours. I came closer to them, crawled right up so my breath fogged their glasses, and saw their fear and disgust silence them as I shone under rage and disfigurement.

Then, as I barked towards a climax, a force caught me from my left and sent me sprawling to the right. I landed in the dirt of the ring. Blood filled my eyes, my head cut by the massive paw that struck me. I heard the screams of the crowd as they dispersed in terror. I saw a black mass of fur sweep the tent into a hurricane as the bottom seemed to fall out of the world and I dropped into the caverns of unconsciousness.

11

'Master thinks I should fight a bear,' the world's strongest boy told the tamer many years before my arrival.

'I think you'll be killed,' said the tamer.

'I'm going to have Leopold fight a bear,' said the master. And so it was.

The tamer recalled what happened to Leopold with less his stare, a broken sentence here or there. Under gibbous moon the tamer called 'I tried to warn him,' and tears formed around his broiling eyes. He called it not to me, although I was the only listener and it was a part of his tale. A whiteness had formed in the corners of his mouth and as he spoke he spat.

When pushed the bear stood up on its back legs like a man. A chain linked its leg to something heavy and that ugly metal snake slunk through sand behind it. It was as tall as two of him, but still Leopold did not look like a child beside it. His arms were thick and joined his neck in a weave of twitching muscles. His legs were longer maybe and thicker where the ball of his knee sat in its nest of tendon, might, and flesh. He stood without a man's sense, the bear before him lacking man's moral code, both degenerate things of common conditions.

Looking like Leopold's vast shadow thrown across the ring by stage lights, the bear roared a sound that broke in the air around it with the feel and pitch of bricks. It dropped again to its forelegs and padded in the dirt, tore up clouds of dust and left tracks in it with his claws like wounds inflicted by the cutting blades of great machinery.

'Two of God's most magnificent creations,' said the master to the crowd. Leopold tensed visibly, arched shoulders and boxed fists, 'put upon each other at last for you, dear audience.' Someone struck the bear with a cane from behind and it raised itself again and threw its arms about in anger or fear or in both. 'We have Leopold, the world's strongest boy. I found him, he won't mind me telling you, in the streets of Paris. Pawing through rubbish in despair, I took him out of there. *Puanteur! La mauvaise odeur!* I cleaned him up, from the kindness in my heart, and when I looked at him again I looked upon a work of art. He'd been killing *chiens* to live. That's *dogs* to you and I. He'd hold a skull in each great hand, and squeeze until they died. I polished him like brass or gold and what I got you now behold, a boy so grand, so strong, so bold, so as to lift a car with strength untold, lift a train, lift whatever your mind can entertain. Now, and only now, from Paris and despair, the strongest boy on earth, he fights *the bear*.'

At that the noise of the crowd soared and the master smiled teeth like blank playing cards. '*The bear*,' he said, 'is the biggest we've got, and we've seen a lot here. He's the meanest thing to come through this town since syphilis and politics. His heated bate is by design, not chance or fate. Not the paltry feels of men but the primal angst of the wild monster, the great, insufferable anger of tyrants that only bones and blood can ever abate. I've seen him eat metal. Eat railway sleepers. Eat deep and full the insides of rotting animals so as to unsettle the toughest gut. See him strut in chains. Liquid steel in his veins. *Murder* in his brains. This husky brown shadow is all that is left of a vile, wild, and dying world beyond man's own that we have set to slumber. It will fight our hero, Leopold, the king of man's new jungle.'

Leopold a preternatural monolith, olive skin slick with sweat that caught the stage lights in its beads so that he appeared covered in white and yellow jewels. Under those lights his eyes twinkled too. The bear an eternal thing, downy, dim like a memory, teeth abrasive white emery and showing now, its saliva hanging in spectral silver catanas. Amid the burden of the crowd's weighty roar the bear padded forward and Leopold turned and fled.

'I called out to him, 'run,'' said the tamer to me under waxing gibbous moon one night. "*Run, Leopold,*' I called. My bear had taken after him around the ring. Around in circles like those damned clowns. I wanted to do something but I couldn't act. I felt a dreadful sinking around my stagnant limbs as if my sweat had spread about the floor and turned it to quick sand. I wish it had. Maybe it would have slowed my bear.'

Cornered and alone, Leopold shook in the shadow of the wood's lost son. One heavy strike from its great paw put him down in the sand and the crowd in a silent trance. Leopold's body trembled, severed from something not physical but frail and divine and dead now. A woman screamed then everyone began absonant and angry. The master, spoke the tamer, had fallen to his knees, people a blur around him.

The master was the conductor of Leopold's recovery. 'His medical knowledge was limited,' said the tamer, 'maybe more so than mine. Somehow the poor boy survived.'

His muscles faded. His veins slimmed, pumped less. His lungs, greasy paper bags that rattled in his rehabilitation, left him with a deep cough, dried and shrunk and held less air. His skin sagged empty as his body receded inwards, hugged weak and slowly healing bones, then tightened, hardened, and in time grew stretched and course and yellow with age.

His face, which was but a torn cloth of skin and sinew, a bloody rag, healed little, merely stopped gushing, crusted, toughened, took on a pinkish hue where scar tissue joined leaves of skin together into what might resemble a face.

That transformation brought about the Leopold I knew, a broken man of only questions.

12

That great big red and white striped tent was empty but for a single light, and five very different figures.

I was one of them, and had just awakened in a state in the dirt. I swam through viscous night, searching out the figures in the dim stage light, my gashed head a ball of agony. I found my way on hands and knees to the feet of the first figure. He murmured something to me through the treacle air. I quivered about his ankles, took him by the trouser legs, and pulled myself up.

It was the master. When he spoke again the air seemed thinner, and I was able to fumble around his words.

'Welcome back,' he said. 'Let go of my trousers.' I removed my hands from him and dropped again to the ground. A second figure helped me up, and I recognised him as the bear tamer. I saw the man was crying. Behind them both, almost in the shadows, rocked Leopold. I could almost not see him, but could hear the sounds of his trapped and liquid breath, and the sobbing muted beneath crossed arms.

There was a smell in the tent then, a deathly smell, the smell of burning flesh and hair.

'I thought,' said the master, 'you would like to see the revenge I've dealt for you.' I wondered whether the blood in my eyes and my lessening concussion were preventing me from seeing clearly, or whether the air was full of smoke. Yes, it was. The smell made my lungs stutter and itch. 'Everything costs something, and that attack has cost this bear his life,' he continued.

There was a thumping diesel generator, almost the size of me. I followed its wires through the dust, piecing together their destination in my mind before I even saw it. At a point in the dirt they split into several finer wires, and disappeared inside an iron cage full of shadows. When they emerged it was to turn to clasps like metal fists and bite deep into the patchy, smouldering fur of a dead black bear. The creature lay with its back to me, as if it had turned away to sulk.

I was overcome by the pain in my skull, and felt crippled by weakness. I fell to the ground, out cold.

There were no longer many bears left on our aisle. They were an endangered species, and went unused in the shows where they had once been copious crowd favourites.

I recovered quickly, and was only absent from the stage for a month.

'You're lucky,' Tick had said, 'I've seen a bear smaller than that tear a man's face clean off.'

When I re-joined the show we had left the beach town and travelled significantly far north by rail.

13

We left the beach and passed through gingham patchwork plains of the yellow-green blurs of corn and deep beige acres of wheat and the sickly smell and blinding yellow suns of rape seed. After, miles of untamed bush and shrub that made up the marshes where men had only been to lay rail tracks. The train was stopped occasionally by the encroachment of the wilderness; its axles throttled by weeds and its incumbents hacking away at them with old blades and sweated brows.

After, hard mountains that maybe shuddered at the sight of us or maybe it was the train's heavy wheels going over a stick or crushing the spine of something tiny and unseen.

As they had risen up upon the earth's horizon, the mountains now passed beside us then fell away black in shadow at our backs as the sun set with them over wherever it was we had been.

At night we travelled so dark I thought I made to see the sounds of our wheels on tracks turning and clicking and great engines burning. They swelled about my eyes in a mechanical maslin that was an ethereal affront to the stars. More stars than I dared to count. The night as if all the things of earth had turned to light and raced away together leaving us tumbling blindly through their void.

Somehow the sun moved always fully beneath us and came again as expected.

In time we rode through a dry land of heat and white sand where that sun rose too soon and too heavy and the tin walls of the boxcars became too hot to touch and reeked the smell of burning paint. I imagined we left a trail of melted colour through the canvas sands, diluting the black pen-line of the tracks and whatever empty page of earth this was.

Atop a higher plain I counted four separate storms on each distance that seemed to circle us like aerial grey wolves. At the bellies of their clouds rains pulled down inky vines that ran through the watercolour sky like paint or the giant tentacles of some great, immobile monster able only to groan and rumble in the distance and thrash its gossamer limbs in tectonic rhythm.

Then again into milder climate. The train that had run hot and loud cooled and turned its great mechanisms in a smoother motion.

When the light rain came those who could open their windows did so. They collected water in beakers and pushed their heads out into the wind and let the pinches of water dampen their hair and take some of the sweat and grit that had dried there.

As we swept further up the country the weather grew bitter and dark. We passed through snowfall that covered mile after mile brilliant white, and through dirty, industrial towns. There the snow turned black with soot and shit.

During my recovery I had dreams of the electric bear. I dreamed him once as a mechanical beast, cogs and gears naked, able to fry anyone he caught in his lightening claws.

Another time I dreamed him burning on a pyre. He was cooked unrecognisable, losing anything visibly animal until he was but a charred skeleton of twisted metal wires, his skull just a rock. His brain, I thought, must have been boiled down to nothing by the flames, its gas eloping with the wind. How strange such a thing could evaporate on a puff of smoke.

The tamer was not physically injured, but was not the same. A part of his brain had been boiled along with the bear's by the pain of watching his favourite things die over and over and over. I tried once to comfort him and failed.

'I can talk to the bears, you know,' the tamer said to me. It was during a brief stop on our journey. We sat around a fire. He swayed a little, squinted one eye. He spoke with the monotone seriousness he used to carry with him everywhere, except now he slurred his words. He let them fall from his sagging lips, not caring where they landed or who picked them up. 'We talk about all sorts of things,' he said.

'Really? What do they say?' I said. He didn't look at me, but to the barred train carriage that held his last two bears. They slept, as maybe he should have too.

'O, they don't talk back,' he said.

Eventually the collage of empty landscapes stopped, and the silhouettes of buildings began to rise up upon the horizons. Our next show was in one of those industrial towns where the railways we'd travelled on seemed as natural and vital as veins. Men shuffled about with their eyes pointing just ahead of their toes. They rarely spoke but when they did it was different. They slanted certain vowels, and skipped many consonants, adding new ones in all the wrong places. I found them hard to understand, and found this new place frightening.

My return to the stage was uneventful. I had been a little nervous but eased under the hatred of the crowd. They were particularly violent. They called me words that I had never heard before, but sounded crude and angry. I hated those people then, for that time I was in the ring. I took that feeling and turned it into my performance. I ran circles around the ring, snapping at the legs of those in the front row, leaving a trail of dust caught in the stage lights. They kicked and tried to trip me, and I snarled and scared them back into their seats. I took a rain of missiles on my back and shoulders, and barked and threw things back. Eventually I was tripped by the master. He put his right boot on my stomach and pinned me to the floor. I was dragged from the stage, fingernails leaving a trail in the dirt, howling through that cavern. The crowd loved this, and chanted my name. My anger left and I felt a contentedness, beginning to understand a little of the feeling of satisfying a crowd.

'That Caliban was really something,' I heard a child say to his father after the show from beneath the bleachers. I'd loitered there as the tent emptied and deflated, and caught what chipped and broken conversation I could. 'I've never seen anything like him. He's disgusting.'

14

From there we travelled into the city. We took a long train journey through hilly, snow-covered countryside. The train was made up just of us. It was old and it was rusty and the paint on its walls was peeling. Once bold and read letters lined carriages' outsides and read 'Husher and Trask', now they simply said 'Hush'.

As we crept out of a valley the city appeared from the hills. It dominated the new horizon like a black mountain range. It must, I thought, have seen us before we spotted it. It must have followed our winding through the snow since we left the town of my birth. As we approached it grew to a size unimaginable, and we burst its skin, became consumed by a forest of concrete. The train continued for a while apace. At one time we rode a bridge above the buildings and the streets appeared as canyons. Another we dropped below the ground and saw nothing beyond our barred windows.

Despite it feeling as though we'd travelled deep into the city, when we stopped we were still near its outskirts, such was its size. The train slowed for a time, then pulled into a freight yard, a cemetery of empty carriages and broken engines covered by a spider web of train tracks. It was late at night and bitterly cold. I couldn't decide if this was the final stop on every line, or a waiting place for those with no destination. Either way, we unloaded and built our camp right there.

I held the light and was hence the eyes through which all men saw. I distributed my gaze evenly about the circus' assembly, and would bend it and chase the voices calling me from the darkness.

Someone had built a fire to keep away the chill and about it they built the tent in the night in the rain. Their shapes moved across the fire often indistinguishable from one another, silhouettes joined by what they carried between them. When my light caught their eyes they appeared as big cats' glowing back at me and often they snarled and bit at the cause of their blindness.

The tent's frame went up first, old and split wooden beam upon beam until its shape stood erect and skeletal and men climbed down from its peak and others began to lash its swaying legs to the ground.

Among them was the master, a figure recognisable from the others for its resemblance to the frame whose building it had overseen again and again. His shadow was the longest and the most still. He stood in the middle of the tent and watched men swing about in its rafters, head tilted back and a hand on his hat. He stood before the fire and I could see that he was sodden from the rain. His shirt clung to his chest and his muscles were taught. He had removed his jacket and rolled up his sleeves, a costume for lifting and carrying but no building he did. The master remained in the middle of the tent as it went up in the rain around him, grin lit by flames beneath.

I shone my light upon the unfolding of the red and white canvas skin. Twenty men surrounded it after its unfurling and they helped it along as ropes hauled it across its bones. Half way over the wind caught and it ballooned out beyond the reach of my torch and the firelight, its end hidden in the night beyond us as if it had no peak and went on forever. It bucked in the wind and dragged the twenty men through the dirt. One fell on his front and called out as his rope ran through and left his hands. He brought the burned things to his mouth. A section of the tent escaped the men, flapping. Another man was carried through the air some feet from the ground, only to land and stumble and pull the canvas back from where it had tried to escape.

Among them was the tamer, drunk and joking and singing to the men around him. He too had lost his jacket and let his shirt cling slick about the old and ropey muscles of his chest and back. 'Sing with me,' he shouted to those who could hear above the wind. '*Haul* together now.'

The canvas was heavy with water and growing muddy from its contact with the ground. The men struggled with it and I provided my light for them the best I could. It was often not good enough, and they chastised me for my apparent lethargy.

After a time struggling they brought the tent up over the frame and tied it down. It shook in the wind. One side pressed in on itself in a great depression until the final rope pulled it rigid and it stood as it would for the next few days.

The tamer moved away with the others to set himself up for the night. The master remained within it. I did not see him come out.

15

Up there, where everything was covered nightly with thick sheets of snow, morale grew thin and drink a thick blanket. The clowns and I were no exception, and completely our moods turned grey as the skies above our heads. Often we drank wine in silence, my hair frozen to my face in icy clumps, and spent the night huddled together to keep warm.

Most nights, after more than a few drinks, we stumbled to the tent to perform our show. We left our scrapyard campsite and crossed maybe a dozen sets of rail tracks. We used an opening in a leave-less, thorny hedge to pass into a field, big and black. The gap in the bushes, explained Pockets, was probably forced by people without homes and animals.

The field held the tent. During the day I could see that some deer or wild horses had made themselves a meal of all the grass and left only brittle yellow patches. I wondered how grass could grow here to feed an animal. Concrete rose up on either side and hid almost all the light other than for an hour or two around midday and only if the sun were lucky enough to burn through all the smog. I knew it was there though, even when I couldn't see it, lighting up the rest of the world. I missed the countryside then, although I only saw it through the bars of train windows. I missed the beach too, where I could watch the sun set over the ocean for hours a day.

The tent in the mud in the day was a depressing sight. At night it was different. The lamp lights that glowed from within and the fairy lights that littered the field, streamed between poles, wrapped in spirals around the big wheel, the flashing coloured bulbs hugging signs advertising every conceivable fancy, threw their light across the field, pitched, bounced, and missed divots and hoof prints, dappling the green-brown desert with rainbows. They threw their colours across the concrete walls as revenge for the death of the sun, and span them about in dizzy patterns. I wondered if this was the only colour in all the city.

People poured from the shadows of the concrete. Hundreds of them gathered in the tent and in the field. They were drunk and violent, like the edges of the ring were made of mirrors. The people there loved to see the freaks. They shouted for us in curiosity and a trailing disgust. They cheered us in admiration as we went about horrifying them with skill and arrogance. I had been damaged by audiences before, when I was first in the aisle, when I was petrified, wrought to whines and cries, the crowds destroyed me, tortured me with their noise. The master, the professional showman that all audiences took him for, was always calm. He always read his crowds and directed them accordingly, guiding their noise like a shepherd. He read his acts and attacked them appropriately. He drove at us like dogs. I had learned to control a crowd, to deal and barter with their desires. By the time we got to the big city the master bayed me with upturned chairs, pointed walking sticks and stabbing heels, and we put on a real show. Those crowds preferred illusion to despair.

'I think God is testing me,' said the tamer as he passed me by one night.

'I think that means he still believes in you,' I said, and the tamer was gone.

16

From the circus to the city, Pockets, Tick and I. A few nights after arriving we committed a rebellious act. The three of us left the circus at midnight and slid between the buildings, drunken. 'Let's take this party further,' Pockets had said, 'people, drink, and wonder lie ahead.'

The city rose around us as an iron hive. Its streets were narrow sewers, bored through concrete mountains. We scuttled down them, the clowns ahead and unobservant, me reading the place as if it were written in Braille. We came to a row of high chimneys rooted in a groaning factory. The factory hummed with the metronomic sounds of machinery. Fingers rose from it impossibly, encasing the sky in the green-black secretion of their tips. More factories followed, and towers I did not recognise. I felt the clowns could not possibly know a path through these streets, and made an extra effort to keep up with them, preferring to be lost in company. The night's sky, occasionally seen, was stained orange and smeared green.

The clowns either failed to notice, or did and didn't care, that we passed two men fighting in the street. They were positioned under a streetlamp which gave the fight a staged appearance, as if it were a competition. The men wore ripped clothing, either damaged by the fight or from a hard life. A girl would sometimes try to get between them, and they'd both yell at her to get out of the way. She cried and waved her arms to no effect.

The most aggressive of the men was earless, metal hanging from his face at several points, rings and studs of silver. His skin was glossy and inked with things unreadable for the movement of his arms as he threw his punches. His head was bald but not from age and ink resided there too, above eyes that were small and already bruised and closing.

The clowns were not the only ones to ignore the fighting pair. People passed them without looking up. When one man was on the floor people stepped over him. When they were throwing punches, people moved around them without a glance.

One of the men fell to the ground, losing a few teeth on the curb. The woman screamed and went to help him up, only to be restrained by the bald, tattooed man, who smiled a bloody simper.

Why, I thought, have I come out and into this?

We passed them on the other side of the street and I walked close to the clowns as we did. I tried not to look at the blood following us down the road.

After a time I felt we passed through a change and the buildings seemed to fall back towards the ground and thin out over it. Here the city was slightly more alight. I recognised shops and houses, their windows yellow and bright. There were more people here, too, always travelling in different directions to each other. They covered ground quickly, eyes ahead of them. The clowns were at odds with them, moving slowly and with almost no purpose, they shouted and sang and made every small patch of light – wherever windows spilled it – a stage.

I got the feeling we had travelled deep into the centre of the city, or headed far into its outskirts, but when we arrived at the tavern only an hour had passed since leaving the aisle. I concluded that however far we had come we had traversed only a fraction of this place. We must be back by sunrise, I thought, and hoped the clowns would know the way.

17

At first inside things seemed in chaos, until I watched a little closer, peering from behind the clowns, and realised that everything and everyone moved in perfect harmony. The tavern was a sun, and people swung around it like planets, moons, and comets. I took in my surroundings. From outside the place appeared decrepit. Wooden panels with loose nails made its walls, cardboard the most of its windows, all except for one, small and cracked. The roof was iron, a metal chimney pumped out smoke. A sign outside read: 'The Wooden Stove'.

Cigarette smoke rose from every table in dancing columns and drifted in clouds about the ceiling. Gravity worked hard to keep some people from joining the smoke in the rafters as they floated from person to person. The drinks in their hands seemed compelled to rise and fall as frequently and effortlessly as leaves in the wind. The clowns fell immediately into this stream, and floated down its path to the bar, which was no more than boards on sawhorses. They bought me some wine and I sat and watched awhile. 'You,' said one man to another, 'you are my brother,' and they embraced

'I think I like this place,' said Pockets.

'You like anything that's full of booze,'

'That, dear Tick, is why I like you.'

I felt warm to this place also; a wooden chest with golden lining, strewn with happy, drunken jewels. One sidled up to us and shook our hands one at a time with hard squeezes. It was the tattooed man from the fight in the street. Immediately I fell back behind the clowns, afraid. When the man took my hand I was careful not to let him have it for too long, and withdrew quickly. He frowned at me, and I cast my eyes upon the floor. When I glanced back he was smiling an empty mouth of gums and tongue and a brown and sticky looking stuff. His left eye had closed up completely and was red and black and blue.

'The clowns,' he said. 'I've seen you at the circus. Haven't nearly got all that makeup off.' He took his sleeve and wiped Tick's cheek. Then he showed him the white mark it had left on his cuff. 'See,' he said.

Tick smiled, leaned in and strained his eyes. I knew him to be searching through a half-drunk fog. 'I'm not sure you want to see me with my makeup off,' he said. Both men cracked smiles, and Pockets put his arms around their shoulders.

Closer now, I saw the ink about the man's head, but could not understand it still. It was in another language and in shapes that I had never seen. On his arm was inked a snake wrapped around an apple.

'Say,' said the tattooed man, addressing Pockets, 'this one's Caliban, right?'

'Right.'

'I can't believe I almost didn't spot him,' he said, and patted me on the head. 'You're the strangest little man I think I've ever seen. Great show that was. My old man thought it an' all. I'd introduce you, 'cept I dunno where he went,' he said, looking around the room.

The tattooed man had cooed these words and I came out from behind the clowns. A few others by the bar had heard the man and recognised us from the circus. A woman was sat on a bearded man's lap. She whispered in his ear and pointed at me.

'He's an ugly little bastard, isn't he?' the bearded man said back.

'Not nearly as ugly as you,' said the woman, and kissed him passionately. The bearded man raised his glass to me across the bar.

Pockets poured the tattooed man a drink and topped up mine. He told us his name was Cole, and that he had no job. 'Anytime you want to come by and say hello, I'll most likely be in 'ere,' he said.

'The greatest show on earth, they call you lot, don't they? Well, I can see why after what we witnessed,' said Cole. Music had started up from a band in the corner and sent vibrations through my bones and left me shifting in my seat. Others danced. The clowns, Cole, and I drank and talked. 'I'd never seen a bear before. And you boys, you two, you made us all laugh. I asked my old man, I said, 'why do you think one of the clowns got a happy face and the other a sad one?' He just shrugged his arms. Then you fell over Tick with that bucket and we all split our sides.'

'He's the happy one,' said Pockets, 'and I'm the sad one.'

'It doesn't make a lot of sense, though,' said Tick, 'as we're both sometimes happy and sometimes sad, and only ever at the same time.'

'Fellas, I can't tell you apart. Even now up close.'

'I know what you mean,' said the clowns in unison.

'What was I saying? Never seen a bear before the greatest show on earth. And Caliban, Primitive Man. I love it. Makes me feel like a monkey again, seeing you runnin' about. I can't believe I'm having a drink with you, really. Can't believe you come in here and drink jus' like me. And the master, ay? What a man. See, when I make something of myself – an' I will, jus' soon as I like – he's the sorta man I'll be; one that commands respect and one with confidence and charm. We've got a lot in common, really, me and the master.'

He leaned in close, and his voice dropped to a whisper. 'See, I'm too *good* for round here, really. I ought to be *in charge*, or something, of something.'

'Why aren't you?' I said.

'I've got a lot of *stuff* going on,' he said. 'Besides, I'm that sort of man, and you can't change that. There are two types of men, and I'm one of them, and you can't change that. Only reveal which one you were all along. And I will. Jus' as soon as I've sorted all this *stuff* out.'

A too familiar pool, we sank to the very bottom of drunkenness so that even the guitar music sounded as though it had travelled through a wall of water. It reached me melted full of bass. I danced, at first with the clowns, who spent most of the time mopping each other off of the floor. Then I danced with the large lady who had pointed at me earlier. I couldn't see the bearded man, but he could have been anywhere amidst a thick and unfocused crowd.

Dancing was my favourite thing right then. I stopped acting as if I had a body, and my arms and legs came to life. Energy ran without thought through my muscles and unlocked my limbs from my mind and I did wonderful things. I held the woman tight close to me, and saw she was ugly. Then I let her dance away a little and saw that how she moved was the most beautiful thing and I danced back so close I could smell the sweat in her armpits. Later she was gone. At first I cared and then I didn't. I went to urinate in a small room at the back of the tavern. Carved above the toilet, next to a patch smeared brown, was a poem that read:

> The women of The Wooden Stove,
> Will teach you more than you can learn.
> They'll kiss your neck with lips so cold,
> And very soon your piss will burn.

At dawn only the clowns and I were left in the tavern. The barman switched off the lights, which shook me from my dreaming. The place was tiny in the dark, and I thought it remarkable that it had held so many only minutes before. The one window, small and cracked, allowed a little light in from the sunrise and The Wooden Stove seemed an empty shoebox, pricked by a pin at one end. Pockets, Tick and I got up and left.

18

'Do you remember,' said Pockets, 'where we first met?'

'I barely remember this morning,' said Tick.

'We were twelve.'

'We were?'

'We were. In that home, remember?'

'Where he found us and put us to work?'

'That's the one,' said Pockets. 'I don't remember much of what happened to me before the home.'

'I don't remember anything that happened to you before the home,' said Tick.

'That's because we hadn't met.'

'It's hard to imagine.'

'Hard, but not impossible,' said Pockets. 'I remember a few things. I remember my mother used to put me to bed every night.'

'Then she died and that pleasure became mine.'

'She used to put me to bed every single night until she died. I remember at the funeral there was this man, I'd seen him at our place once or twice, always late at night, but had never spoken to him. At the funeral he came up to me and said, 'Bloody shame about your mum, sunshine, she was one 'elluvawoman.' He had teeth like broken bricks.

'After that I was in that tiny house for a week on my own before I met you, and I shook every time I put myself to bed.'

'Shook?'

'All night. I almost shook my bed apart. They were convulsions I had no control over, and I shook as if it were freezing cold. My teeth would even chatter. I tried to relax, tried to let every part of me fall asleep one by one. I'd focus really hard and get my right leg still, but as soon as I moved my attention to the left, the right would start up shaking again. It seemed like there was nothing I could do to stop it, and I'd shiver and weep myself to sleep.'

'You've *shaken* my memory, Pockets. I remember now, you quivering in your bed.'

'How could you, you weren't there?'

'At the home.'

'Oh, at the home. Yes, it carried on there, too. Then it stopped when we joined up with the master.'

'Just like that?'

'Just like that. I found a cure you see, after all those years, for the lonely shakes.'

He took a long drink from a bottle of clear spirits, emptying it. "Elluvawoman,' he said, and went to bed.

19

A few days later the clowns and I made our way back into the crevices of the city. The idea was to reach The Wooden Stove once more. I felt we crept about for lifetimes, lost, but again misjudged the clowns' noses. Sure enough, we came upon the pooling light and wicked sight of The Wooden Stove.

A wicked sight. That night it finally came to me what we were, the clowns and I and all the rest that had been sheltered from the real world, just as paccant and bruised as ours, by a great big red and white striped tent. We were creatures, nothing more. Maybe less but nothing more. And so were they, the audience, the shadowed unseen heads that bayed and booed and cheered and laughed, under tent and under stars. But we were not theirs and they not ours. Some thing, appearance, vice, or otherwise, had pitched us apart as two sides of a dirty coin. They viewed us, I saw, as monsters.

Three people were hanged from their necks outside The Wooden Stove. The bartender, Cole, and the woman who danced with me. A sign was painted on each of their chests. 'We associate with beasts,' it read.

Tick sobbed the journey back and Pocket led the way. I stayed behind the two, as usual, and tried to piece together what I had seen. I held myself tight and kept a good pace with the clowns, peering down every street and around every corner. I wished I were back at the beach or, better yet, still in the ground.

When we returned the master was waiting by our caravan. He sat on a canvas chair he must have brought himself. One slender leg crossed over the other, his floating boot rocking softly in the air. A book rested open across his lap. He wore thin rimmed, small lensed reading glasses that made him look older than the old man he already was. A lamp hung from the canvas porch just beside him so that he sat in a glow.

The clowns didn't fright at the sight of him. Tick carried on sobbing, and Pocket stood there waiting, staring at his feet.

'Go to bed,' said the master to the clowns, and they did, disappearing quickly out of sight. I went to follow, but was blocked by an outstretched boot. The master patted his jacket until he found what he was looking for in his breast pocket and pulled out a cigarette, lit it with a match. 'Not you,' he said, and released a cloud of smoke from between his lips.

'Let me explain this to you, my boy, so that I can go home and go on reading. I have plucked you, your clown friends too, from the sewers of the world. Not a nice world, granted, but a world that flushed you all as soon as it lay a squinting, repulsed eye on you. You washed up here, at my feet. I am your go-between. This is hell, out there an empty purgatory, and I am Charon. Enjoy the ride. Make yourself comfortable. There is no way back and even if there was they'd never accept you. They hate you even before they know you, because you are an evil looking thing.'

'I do not accept that.'

'What did you see in that city?'

'Three people killed.'

'More than that? What about the other night?'

'Dancing, drinking, joy. A fight.'

'A fight. And more?'

'And people like I've never seen before.'

'Did they scare you?'

'Not then.'

'They were fighting, laughing at you. They'd have hurt you had they not known me as your protector.'

'They would not hurt me.'

'They will get you like they got your friends from that tavern.'

He rose, placed the book open on the canvas chair and stretched. He turned and left. As quickly as he was absorbed into the night, Leopold arrived, hunched. Without a word he took up the master's book, folded up his chair, and carried them after.

The tamer told me heaven is above us. If that were true, I thought, then we most certainly are in hell.

20

I dreamed I was the nightmare of a child. I dreamed that my mother came to say goodnight to me after I had climbed into a bed so soft and warm. She pulled my blanket up above my chin so only my eyes peeked out above. They looked up at her and moistened. She looked back, smiled, kissed my forehead, smooth and pale and utterly normal. My fingers wriggled out from beneath the covers and I felt her hair and kissed her back.

In my dream I lay awake a while, listened to my parents, never seen before, shift and slide about the rooms below. That faint noise was a lullaby. At the circus the night is silent but for occasional howls and bangs and clatters that would jolt me from dreaming and send me upright, starring wide-eyed and afraid.

I slipped beneath another layer of sleep and the me that lay in a bed as big as the clowns' whole trailer had the severe and lucid nightmares of a child. I found myself in the circus ring. I watched the dark crowd that formed a full circle around me, but saw they were at odds with me; the low barrier and few feet of dust a thousand miles of differences. I looked down at my hands and was shocked to see the cracked and scaly skin. If I were to pick at it I'd pick myself apart. There was rain, carried by the wind, and it made its way easily into the tent.

I could find no shelter from it. It rapped on the tent's walls and a globule of sweat fell sticky on the floor and met the sand and formed a tiny crystal of what looked like glass. Then it dried into nothing under the heat of the lights that had wrung it from my skin in the first place. I watched another pad of sweat form and dry in the dirt. Then another, until like the outside clouds I beat my deluge on the ground. The crowd drubbed their sound upon my back. They threw their shots on skin that time and shows had used and cracked. A back that was black and blue and bruised and on my head came an open wound. My skin was sand through fingertips. I had no ears no nose no lips and behind my eyes the distant lights of passing midnight ships who had but the ocean and at that a fading memory of it. A name that was not my name, all that wretched fame and an ever fading memory of all of it.

Under the heckles of the crowd I was rushed into the night by fantastically costumed freaks. Painted smiles and wild eyes bobbed atop cloths of dizzying colours and patterns. Hands smothered me, touched my broken skin and rushed me away from the tent. A drizzle travelled horizontally through the air, propelled by a wind that swelled and billowed their cloths and tugged painfully cold at my nakedness. I refrained from struggling and held myself against the elements, allowed myself to be ushered into darkness.

I was thrown to the ground beneath a low canvas tent where two evil clowns bickered in a language I didn't understand. They snatched at a bottle, growled at me and turned back to fighting.

Thunder and lightning hit once, at once, and I woke into that soft, dark room screaming under my blanket.

The shuffling from below turned to quick footsteps on stairs, and both my mother and my father came into my room.

'There, there,' said my mother, kissing my forehead again.

'It's all right, son,' said my father. He moved through the darkness, and as he switched on the light I woke up in my bed in the aisle.

The circus quit the big city. We performed one more show after the three were hanged, a disappointing performance, claimed the master.

'You killed three people in this town with your collective evil, but you can't put it to work when it really counts,' he said after, having brought us all into the tent to debrief and degrade.

We left unspectacularly, keeping our eyes forward, not watching the city sink like a giant ship into the horizon. It was a sight when we rolled towards it. We'd crept up feeling like such tiny things in its massive shadow. We left feeling just as small, but for different reasons. I could not help but think about the three, tiny like we. I wondered if I were the only one whose mind they hung on in that innominate labyrinth of factories, towers, and shadows. I thought I probably knew them best of all, even though their names and faces were departing on a train in another direction, as I rode the master's train, descending, and they floated upwards, already nothing more than a breeze.

The clowns moved on from our ordeal quickly, forgot the three like I was trying desperately to. We rode the train for days and they returned to normal within one or two – or as normal as they could be; a soup of sorrow, drink, and calamity.

I wondered why the master had only spoken with me when we returned from our second visit into the city. The clown's resurgence told me they had heard it all before. They had known their place, faltered through drink and friendship's ambition, and settled back into the comfort of the great big red and white striped tent. I wondered what other horrors the clowns had known lying further back by the sides of our train's track, but decided not to ask.

We headed further north, I was told, towards the top of the land where all that lay beyond was water, ice, and sunken ships. We were on the train again for only days, but we passed through seasons. Spring broke out of the windows, and melted snow fed green fields. Then darkness and winter painted everything monochrome and we passed through every hue of grey.

I let the time by silently in a carriage on my own, eating and sleeping. I made myself a bed of old coats and straw on the train's hard floor, lips parched and cracked, cheeks crusted with dried snot and tears. My carriage was shared with various aisle dwellers over the journey. They came and went. From time to time I'd hear the door at the end of the carriage slide open, and the wind would blow loud and cold. At other times I heard a shuffling, some snoring, quiet words with no replies. I saw little of the clowns, the tamer, the master. We didn't stop once and I never thought to stumble down the shaking passage to find them. But Pocket and Tick must have felt it too. It was brought on by our brief escape, by a fleeting happiness. Wrestling and urgent, it lay wriggling in my gut, begging me to listen. When I turned an ear to the thing inside, it said three words; 'open your eyes.'

When the train began to slow, after what felt to me like a year, I was asleep – I had been sleeping most of the days away. I had been dreaming intensely. That night I had dreamed that there was a darker space in the dark night sky, a patch where no stars dared be. It hung beyond the atmosphere, pinned up against a board of tiny electric lights until I realised that it was not a hole, not a nothing, but a vast sleeping thing that didn't scare off the stars from a space but covered them with its giant form. It hid them from all the curious eyes of millions a million miles away. It grew in the sky, flew down to earth and I realised that it was a giant bird made of a material so dark and empty that I didn't see it, but saw only everything around it. The empty bird became the whole night sky. I tried to ignore it, to concentrate on what I *could* see, but I became lost in the loss of the stars and the moon and its darkness lay over my eyes like a film.

When I woke up I found that I had been staring through the carriage window into the rising sun. Black patches covered the centre of my vision. When they faded so did the deep sadness that had ridden with me since the city, and I found that we were again by a sea.

I felt well rested. It was warm in the carriage, and I was surprised when I opened the door and the temperature didn't drop noticeably. Patches of snow lay on the grass but only in small and scattered blankets. We were in another train yard, cleaner than the one in the city. Our circus engine had pulled up alongside an empty passenger train. Its paint was intact, windows clean and unbroken and reflecting a cloudless morning sky. Next to it ours looked a demonic thing, ridden all the way from hell at breakneck speed. The nicer train had bar-less windows, was painted a bright red. Inside I saw plush seats and clean tables. I thought that it must be a nice way to travel.

We dropped from our carriages and box-cars, feet slapping wet grass and soaking our cuffs. All together the aisle's inhabitants swept the yard, stretching their arms and craning their necks skywards, as if we had all woken up from a hibernation.

We were by the sea again; a different one, yes, but the sea nonetheless. I was pleased to find out that we would not be staying in the train yard, which was still in use, but on the beach. Our circus was booked as part of a spring festival welcoming in the warmer weather and bidding farewell to the snow. I was happy to do the same. It was as strange a place, in many ways, as the city. A miniature version of its cousin's skyline, its sole sky-toucher was a church, I learnt, no taller than the tallest trees. Buildings fewer, with farther space between. We were alone by the beach, our tent joined a slowly building festival by a pier that reached towards the horizon, just missing. Waves kissed it in the distance, and stroked the closer sand by our aisle.

21

'She was a sad woman,' said Pockets.
    'Who was?' said Tick.
  'The mistress.'
  'The mistress of the home?'
  'The old homestead, yes.'
  'What was it she said?'
  "It is a cruel world, that looks so nice,' whilst gazing out of the window, then she'd blow out our light. I never understood that, until I saw the sea.'
  Pocket gestured across the waves with his left, and poked our fire with his right. His hands and sleeves were black with soot. He had some smeared across his face, too, mixed with his makeup.
  'What do you mean?'
  'It's so beautiful, but sink to the bottom, try and have a really good look, and you'll drown.'
  'She sounds a strange woman,' I said, watching the flames dance and embers crack and pitch about them. Pockets nodded, poked the fire again.
  'She was,' he said. 'She never left the house.'
  'Used only candles,' said Tick.
  'That's right. Candles every night. She would read to us by them.'
  'That's right!'

'Stories, sometimes about the sea, but mostly a great hero, sweeping up a fine woman. Stories we had no interest in really, except the girl.'

'I don't remember the girl.'

'And I doubt she remembers you, or I. I doubt she's even still alive. It's a cruel world for someone so beautiful.'

'We're lucky we're ugly,' said Tick. 'I wonder if she thought the master would come and sweep her up.'

'The girl?'

'The mistress.'

'That's right, the master would come and see her late at night. I think maybe she did. What was it, about once a year? We'd hear her moaning upstairs, see his face in the doorframe as he looked at us and said, 'Not yet."

'He swept us away, not her,' said Tick. 'Do you think she cried?'

'She struck me as partial to a cry, yes. She didn't as he took us though, just played with the hem of her blue nurse's dress and floated behind him as he led us out the door. She waved from the porch like a child. Remember what he said to us?'

Tick thought hard then with a grin said, 'A clown is a noble creature, absurdly august. His job is to entertain, yet he remains magisterial and proud, a professional and an artist.'

'Yet I've worn makeup every day since.'

22

They came together as things always do: They were next to each other the whole time, and would be time and time again. When the rain made the stone slick and less stone-like it softened the earth and the stone made a bed as shaped and as smooth as a pistachio shell. When the rain made the stone slick and handsome it made the earth moist too. When the sun dried the stone, warmed it dull, it pulled up the flower from the earth with a warm and beckoning finger of light. From there grew the flower to be with the stone. Stone had stood as long he could remember, flower new and smiling.

One day the sun stopped shining, and the rain doubled its efforts. Then froze. It coated stone a flattering white, flower a terminal weight and darkness. Flower fell away and frozen stone was left alone again. Battered by the rain, he grew flatter and flatter.

We skipped stones by a pond. The clowns showed me how. The water was clear but for the glacial drifting of small patches of ice. As the clowns searched about its edge for a suitable stone I watched a leaf arrive on the wind. It circled the pond with no intent, came down to the surface where the water made a careen of the sky, its low clouds, the branches and stray leaves and our dancing forms. The leaf's round sole kissed the water's skin just before the wind carried it away must faster than it had arrived. I turned my back to the breeze and saw Pockets wheel across the many-coloured pebbles that made for themselves a shelf or shore by the water. He span with a flat stone in his hand and cursed the thing as he let it from his task across the water. It touched the surface once after a few feet, leapt back spinning inches above it, a grey dervish, a squashed and soaring moon above a watching ocean, it broke the surface again, brought up with it a fine spray that tracked itself over and over behind the stone's flight in the shape and intricacy of a peacock's tail. At last its glide was disrupted, it bounced awkwardly and set itself spinning on many more axes, curling right and bouncing higher until it came to a stop with a *plunk* and sank forever. Pockets cheered and Tick looked on unimpressed.

At that sound something hiding in the undergrowth beside us rustled away and the breeze picked up again. It brought the smell of caramel and engine oil.

'You poor man,' said Tick, and cast his flattened stone. He leapt every time it touched the water until it surpassed Pockets' by a single bounce. Tick cheered and waved his arms as his stone joined his friend's beneath their own fading ripples.

'No poorer than you,' said Pockets, 'Neither of us made it to the other side.'

'A single bounce more is still more.'

'Is still poor is all I'm saying.'

There was a noise behind us and it alerted the clowns and I straight away, a crashing through the trees and a coughing. Out of the bush came the tamer. He broke into the small clearing on a stumble and fell straight away to his knees. I saw dirt on him in places and his face was long and pale and bearded. In one hand he clutched an empty bottle. He crawled on all fours across the pebbled shore, made a crunching sound as his knees pushed down, ground and rounded and lifted forward, quivering under their own weight. The bottle, dragged, left a shallow furrow in the pebbles. The clowns parted either side of the tamer with slow backwards paces, and he passed between them beneath their mouths slightly open and their staring eyes. When he got to the edge of the water he sunk the bottle entirely beneath it and knelt there panting and waiting. The bottle emptied its emptiness into the pond, and air bubbled to the surface. With his other hand the tamer began to cup water and dash it on his face. He rubbed his hand through the folds of skin about his neck then repeated this unsure cleaning.

Long after the bubbling had stopped the tamer took the bottle from the water and began to drink great gulps, letting it pour around his chin and return to the pond in uneven foaming streams.

'You poor man,' said Tick.

'No poorer than you,' said the tamer, and spat into the pond. He wore a dirty straw boater hat, the ribbon gone.

He stood up, greeted us all individually by shaking out hands. Then he sat beside me and crossed his legs. He took another swig of water then dug his bottle into the pebbles so that it sat up of its own effort.

'Sit down with me,' he said. 'I'm tired.'

I joined him on the pebbles. The clowns started up skipping stones again, and the tamer and I watched.

'I've beaten you,' said Tick. 'That means the drinks are on you.'

'What drinks? Where are they on me?'

'Don't clown.'

'My dear Tick, drinks usually are on me. You're such a glass half empty sort of chap. I'm the one who keeps your glass half full.'

'I –'

'–do your best to empty it, I know, you miserable thing. Watch my throw,' Pockets ran across the pebbles, almost broke into a cartwheel as he let one arm arc about his person at full distance. The released stone bounced once more than Tick's.

'You're the winner, then,' said Tick. 'That means the drinks are on you.'

The tamer watched their exchange, his forehead wrinkled and breath low.

'What is this fantasy land?' he said. 'What is this place you've created for yourselves that so transcends the faecal matter in which you really lay, because you lay in faecal matter and blood like newborns?'

'We may live in filth but at least it's our own' said Pockets.

'Something to call our own,' said Tick.

'Shit is shit,' said the tamer. 'Animals live in their own filth. *Bears* do not, incidentally. Bears can go whole winters without defecating. If you leave a bear alone, just leave him alone, he won't *die* like we would die. He'd take off through the trees and he'd be fine.'

'We could do that,' said Tick. 'If we wanted to.'

'You came from the trees, and I don't see that you'll go back. You came through the tree line, one after the other, a jilted and tiny diaspora.'

'I don't remember at all where we came from,' said Tick.

'No makeup. No shadow as it was midday,' said the tamer. 'It was dusty and hot. The kind of dusty that distorts the heat in front of you and it looks like your whole caravan is headed into a land of fire.

The tamer paused, pushed his bottle further into the pebbles then looked up at the clowns. He let his eyes rest on them.

'You looked no different from now, really,' he sighed and returned his watch to the pebbled shore on which he sat. 'You came from the treeline fifty feet ahead of where I was. It can't have been more than that. You first,' the tamer pointed at Pockets. 'Then Tick. You came out the easiest, stepped over a thorny curb of bull nettles and ocotillo. Or was it nettles and dead holly? Some of it clung to the leg of your trouser, which was torn up the inside seam of your left leg. You picked it off, your jowls bouncing below your face as you bobbed on one leg. Then you pulled Tick out from whence you'd come yourself. Tick looked the worse off, bruised and lost and far skinnier than now. You look healthier these days, in some ways, the both of you.

'You looked at each other, and then you just fell in line with us. Pockets there to lean on and Tick with a limp.'

In the jilted trees something rustled leaves. A few fell to the ground. The tamer motioned two men with the first two fingers of each hand. They walked through the air one behind the other.

'You're not the only ones to have arrived just like that. There's been quite a few who have stumbled out of that treeline and fallen in line with homeless brothers, recognised a deep inner sadness beyond the cosmetic tatters that merely say 'I would like something to eat and drink and wash with, and perhaps somewhere to spend the night,' for which there are a thousand men just with that for every man alive in here. There's something different on the other side of the trees for every one of you who make it in here. I don't confess to know your cosmology, clowns, but what was on the other side of those trees could not have been pretty for the looks in your eyes that day.'

The tamer let his gaze fall about the pond where the ice that floated did so still. Three flies skipped over its surface, as did for a moment the slightest ray of light.

'Well,' said the tamer, and got up and left.

'I've had enough of these ghost stories,' said Tick, 'completely enough. I don't think I should have to put up with that. Not one bit.'

Tick picked up the closest stone to him and cast it into the pond, then he turned and went towards the aisle. Pockets followed and I followed too.

23

I'd seen the tamer drift about the aisle since his pack had dwindled beyond recognition. His arms always hung loose at his sides, the weight of his balled fists looked the only thing stopping him from floating away like a child's lost balloon. His chest had caved in, empty, and his eyes burned with hurt and focussed on nothing. He became increasingly dirty and unkempt. People stayed away from him. His segment of the show had been erased, replaced by an extended trapeze performance. The last two bears, just as dirty as the tamer, knocked about their cage as nostalgic ornaments to one of the circus' longest serving acts, waiting to be forgotten completely and thrown away. The duty of feeding them had been passed on, their new keeper uncaring and their old an abstract, animal memory. If they missed him it was in the same way that they missed the faraway forests of their youth; a fleeting and ambiguous image that might occasionally obscure the eye like a bacterium. I was sure, after I saw the bottle, that he missed them, and missed those forests for them.

Word spread about the aisle quickly, and came to me through the clowns. The story went as follows:

The evening was the farthest rings of rippled water; it was well and truly night. The tamer stole an eyeball full of his cherished bears in secret, as he often did, and moved away without catching their attention. Whiskey had softened his perfect diction, and although he spoke constantly not a sound came out. He moved his lips in silence, and had no idea what noises he'd be making if he could. His smell would have repulsed him if introspection was still within his grasp. Instead, avoiding everyone, he moved from thing to thing and viewed them like a lizard, silent and scared.

He was still capable of basic emotion, and could oscillate between crests and troughs of feeling with the impulse of animals. One moment he stared delirious at the moon and smiling tried to touch it. Another, anger fermented inside of him as he watched people he knew but didn't come a little too close.

To him the aisle was a playground of shadows and shapes and he dove between them on unsure legs. He found himself beneath the big wheel, its lights off and its bulk still. He sat and finished off a bottle, relaxed, and wet the ground around him without realising. Just as he readied himself for sleep, two men alerted him, and he became suddenly aware of himself. One was small and cowardly, brought a little consternation, but moved like a deer and was disregarded. The second was taller, wore a cape that made its form more alarming. It moved closer and its features became clearer. Something about him riled the tamer; the wrinkled face, flowing cape, top hat, and cane; the way he strove and swayed between the shadows, unafraid of the moonlight.

The tamer struggled to right himself, used the metal legs of the big wheel as support, and lunged across the aisle. He came upon the men from behind and let out a cry. Leopold span around first, whimpered and held out his hands to protect himself. The tamer pushed him aside. The master turned too late, and the tamer struck him across his head with the whiskey bottle, splitting the former and smashing the latter.

He stood shaking by the big wheel. The master lay unconscious at his feet, and he began to recognise his victim. The bottle's bodiless neck was still in his hand, which began to quiver and shake as he quickly sobered.

'Please,' said Leopold, 'I don't want to fight.'

At Leopold's begging the tamer and the aisle around him started to wake. He dropped the broken bottle neck and ran. The next few minutes were the clearest his mind had been in a long time. In those lucid moments he went to the bear cage, busted the lock with a stone, and led the last two bears out of the aisle with him.

On hearing this story I thought about earlier and more sober times with the tamer. He had always spoken and acted with such clarity and honesty. One time when travelling between towns we had come together upon a statue. 'Monument to the Last Wolf', it read, and was an animal dipped in iron. It was a cold grey mottled with red spots of rust. The wolf was positioned so as to appear noble. Her forelegs were on a ground slightly higher than the rear, her head angled back so that her jaw, breast, and legs formed a smooth line to the sky. She howled silently at it.

In truth I do not think it was a very noble positioning, cold and dead and still as it was. The pride was that of the sculptor, not the creature's creator. He had made a fine rendering, after killing the last wolf.

The sheep sleep better, no longer spend the nights checking their numbers in case one had been carried away to be eaten.

I was confused. We had had a wolf with us at the circus. His name was Lobo. He was a docile wolf, always hungry, friendly to everyone except the silent things that tormented only him and only at the night's dark peak. To them he'd bare his fangs, drip white saliva in thick and rotten smelling strings, howl and bark until the tamer came to coo and sooth him from his foaming ire.

In the day he'd pad about his cage, waiting for a show like the rest of us. I would sometimes play with him under the watch of the tamer. I would pat him on the head and say 'Good boy, Lobo,' like the tamer had said to, and Lobo would usually fall on his back and show me his balding, pink belly.

I had asked the tamer about the statue. 'The wolf in the statue can't be the last,' I said.

'There have been no wolves for decades,' said the tamer.

'But we have one here,' I said. 'Lobo. You trained him yourself.'

'He's just an Alsatian coloured grey.'

The broken glass, bloodied edges drying slowly in the biting night, was already trodden in the sand and the mud by the time the story reached me. A failed attempt at a rancorous revenge, maybe. I never asked. The tamer's last stand is what it was. Why is either self-evident or not important. They call me, now, a catalyst for what happened to the circus, but that attack was it.

Inside I cheered for him, and upon hearing the news felt immediately alive with energy, but fell back to my usual self when I saw the master, fine and well and angry.

He gathered us in the tent before the opening show of the town's spring festival, needing to be seen standing, needing to be seen victorious.

'No doubt you've heard,' he said, 'that an assassination attempt has been made on myself by one of you.' We all shuffled silently. 'Don't worry yourselves. I am fine, as you can see,' he stretched his arms and kicked his legs, 'and will lead the show tonight.'

There was relief in some quarters, and a muted discord among the rest. The show, as I've heard people say, must go on, I found myself confide with no one.

'And now the consequences,' our master said. 'I ran him out of here myself, blood foaming on my forehead. He proved pathetic game, even for a wounded man. He could barely put one foot in front of the other, and I pursued him casually, sportingly, to the boundary of our popup hamlet. He is on the errand of a fool and the world will have its way with him. It will eat him up and swallow him whole, I have no doubt. Outside our ethereal walls there is no place for the likes of you and him. The people out there know what he tried to do to me, your master. If you look out at the church tower tonight I've no doubt you'll see a sorry, hanging man, put there on my command.'

24

The master, his speech over, tapped his cane in the dirt and the crowd of acts dispersed. The main lights came on, music started up and covered the impatient noise of the waiting audience beyond the tent's thin walls. They quickly filed in and took their seats behind the black curtains the stage lights created. I hated them. I cursed them for what they did in the city to Cole, the bartender and the woman, and for what they were doing to the tamer right then. I saw them as a single being, a sea monster, pulpous body inside the tent, tentacles stretching out across the world, committing evil at their tips, hanging my friend the tamer.

It was then that I reconciled all the brief and transient feelings that had mocked and teased me since my birth. Of friendship and freedom I dreamt. Of the tiny oases of beauty that beckoned from the barren world outside the aisle, and my desire to meet it, to slink between the danger with my allies and see all there was to be seen. To sink to the bottom of the ocean and hold our breath for as long as we could, listen to the echoes around us, then drift to the surface and trade places with the moon. Not to punish the evil doers, the masters and the hangers, but to escape them, and enjoy the chase. Not to oust them and deal them the same hand they dealt us, but to hide forever from their judgement in the fair fountains that I thought must litter that moral desert.

I had only seen fleeting beauty from the barred windows of trains and trucks, sometimes beyond the invisible walls of the aisle, and swore to seek them out. I would shrug off this place, find a disguise if I had to, and make my way around the world.

First, I thought, I would rescue the tamer.

The master introduced me with his usual verve, the only difference a bandage wrapped around his head, reddening when he pushed his voice out louder. He rubbed it sometimes between his lines.

'– and in disgusting surrender, he kissed my leather boots, kissed my ivory cane, swore allegiance to mankind, never to be the same. I caged him, tried to tame him, and now, on stage, my slave – Caliban.'

The shrouded crowd cheered, and I stepped into the spotlight. I didn't growl or claw, didn't bark or bite. I stood in the centre of the ring and stared into the darkness after it. A braveness came across me, better than that which drinking brings, and I spoke.

'You,' I said, 'you are monsters.'

From beyond the gloom, the shadow tapestry that hung on the walls of our cavernous, canvas room, a mumbling started. It rose into a cacophony of voices and sounds, meaning hidden by their overlapping, jaw-flapping selves, an aphonic noise of discontent.

'Quiet,' I said. And they were. 'I am going to church.'

25

'We always have each other,' said Tick, 'no matter what happens now.'

'And we have spirit,' said Pockets.

'We have spirit when we're drinking spirits.'

'Or drinking anything, for that matter.'

They paused.

'Shall we, then?' said Pockets.

'Shall we what?' said Tick.

'Change the planet's course. What else is there to do?'

'Stay.'

'No. No I think we'd better go.'

'How long have we been here now?'

'What, this town? Oh I don't know abou-'

'No, not here. At the circus.'

'As long as I can remember,' said Pockets.

'That's what I was afraid of.'

'What? What were you afraid of?'

'Time,' said Tick.

'Shall we, then?'

'Yes. Yes I think we'd better.'

'There's more wine in the tent, right?'

'We're not going back to the tent.'

'Right.'

'But there'll be more wine.'

'Do you promise?'

'I promise.'

'Everything will be fine?'

'I can't, but I promise there'll be more wine,' said Pockets.

I left the circus with the clowns in pursuit, the tent at my back sounded off with disbelief and disappointment. Somewhere in the noise I imagined was the master screaming, but all of their discontent fuelled me. I took long steps up the beach, pointed my strides at the church tower on the horizon, and felt charged by the thought of a tent full of frustration and anger. They would be after my neck, I was sure, but for the first time in my life I had a head start. When the tent dropped out of sight I could still hear a rabble, but could not see anyone following.

We doubled our speed down deserted streets, cobbled roads easier on the feet than the sand of the beach. The most of the town's people were back at the show. Maybe they would stay and watch the rest, I thought. Whatever the case he would be after me soon enough. I was an escaped monster, not even I knew what damage I intended to cause. I considered briefly turning back and burning them all alive inside the tent. I saw the fiery frame of the thing collapse and bury them all. I saw the black iron of their bones poke through the charred remains of canvas, red, white, and black, the only smoking things left. The image was too clear, and I shook it from my mind.

We walked down the centre of abandoned roads, three in a line and side by side. Words were not shared between us, and in truth I do not think we knew what we planned to do, only that there was not yet a hanging man on that steeple, and we intended there never to be.

A man crossed the road ahead of us to be directly in our path. The clowns stopped and I urged them on. That man has been sent for us, I thought. Beneath his coat is a whistle that he'll blow and these empty buildings will light up like the circus and we will be surrounded.

I pictured pitchforks and flaming torches. I saw the tamer noosed, three more hanging empty and loose in a row beside him, and four signs that read 'we are beasts'. All lit solely by the torches of the townspeople.

As the man approached I saw that he was watching us closely. He held his coat tight to his body and took long steps towards us. As he closed in he eyed me steadily, bowing a little to be closer to my height. Without stopping or slowing he came closer, switched his look to the clowns, standing upright and taller than them as he arrived. Then he stepped around us, faintly smiled, pulled his hat over his eyes and passed us by.

The church was like the most of the town. It sat in an empty space, everyone still at the show or in lazy chase of us. Saint Barbara's Church stood impressive and dark among gravestones. Cold rock blocks piled higher than anything else in the town. It rose almost out of sight. I was relieved to see no man hanging from its spire, just a cross up there among the stars. Trees, a rare thing to be seen, had made an ancient home of its gardens, taller, older, and wiser than the neighbouring houses. A path lay beneath their branches and led to Saint Barbara's closed wooden doors.

I crossed the hall a forsaken thing, the clowns waiting outside, closed doors behind me. They said, arms folded and shaking, that they were to keep vigil and watch for trailing trouble, but their eyes could not be drawn from the severe stone of Saint Barbara's high walls. So I sought the tamer alone, and appeared to be alone still as I stood inside the church. I began taking tiny steps along Saint Barbara's narrow aisle, short and empty pews either side of me. It had few windows, and above and beside me stone pillars supported low, black rafters. I made my way carefully towards an alter covered with bouquets of subtle flowers and many tiny candles, their colour and glow alone in that modest space. My bare feet made no sounds, and I thought I heard the candles flicker.

The alter seemed a natural destination. The church's sole road led only to it, and I felt that I was travelling towards a climax. I thought perhaps I was too late, and that the tamer had been hanged, cut down, and buried unmarked outside before I got there. I thought that the doors behind me had been locked, the clowns murdered, and evil hands were reaching from the darkness between the pews clenching knives.

No hands grabbed me and no blow fell upon my head. I reached the alter shivering but unharmed. If my back were bowed before it was doubly so then, I stood in front of tens of tiny flames and flowers, shielding my naked chest with my arms, and allowed looks only through squints.

'He was here,' said the priest, and I fell back against the floor. 'They took him to the bridge.'

26

We set off again through the town, and by that time were surprised not to have been ambushed.

'We're easy prey,' said Pockets. 'We're fish in buckets. Why would they miss the rest of the show when they can hang us in the morning?'

The bridge was at the edge of the town. It was a tall iron thing that crossed a green river, struts jumbled and rusted. No traffic passed over it. Steep banks held the river, all long grass and mud and sludge.

'They must have drowned him,' said Tick. 'Maybe they filled his boots with concrete and sunk him.'

I was the first over the bank, I started down the muddy hill. My lighter frame made it easy to cling to fistfuls of grass which tore from their roots as I lowered myself to the next foothold. Nettles stung my naked skin which turned red and itched. Pockets helped Tick over, and they came down above me slowly.

After some feet I could see a glow from beneath the bridge. It was the dance of flames on the lower bank, on the bridge's bars and bottom lip. It rode, along with the reflected moon, the gentle current of the river. It painted the green water with yellows, oranges, and reds. All three of us heard a noise then, but could not fully make it out. Laughing, several voices. We saw shadows move about, slicing up the soft light of their owners' fire.

'They'll kill us,' said Tick, and the voices stopped below.

'Who's there?' called one, and we stayed still. Two men, lit from behind, came out from beneath the bridge. One had his arm around the other's neck. The first I didn't know, but the held man was the tamer. He swayed a little.

'Let him go,' I said.

'What?' called the unknown man.

'He is my friend, the tamer, and I will let no harm come of him.' I dropped from the bank, landing at the pair's feet. The clowns called after me but I did not listen. There were four more men beneath the bridge, silhouettes against a burning metal drum. Empty cans and bottles were scattered about.

I made myself as large as I could be at the feet of the man who held the tamer, but still my head barely surpassed his crotch. I arched my back and growled at him, just like I would a crowd. I swiped at the air in front of him, and he took a cautious step back. His eyes flashed down at me, and he straightened himself up.

The clowns appeared behind me and I felt bigger then with my friends at my back. I wanted the strangers to fear me. I was a monster who had escaped from his cage. They could not hide on the other side of a circus ring. I was not in chains or under the boot of the master. I was there, loose in their town. Just as I had a crowd, I used their hate and turned it into fear. I used their fear to forge more hate. I turned at the other men, barked swears and evil noises at them and they cowered.

'Let him go,' I said again.

I sat low on my calves and readied myself to lung at the stranger who held my friend. I would bite at his legs, I thought, pull him to the ground, jump atop him and beat his head against the concrete until his eyes rolled back and his tongue hung out. I would move on to the others and do the same, orgiastic, until the ground pooled with all their blood and we could make our escape.

I pushed off from the ground. Straight away I was knocked back. I landed against the bank and grazed my back against it. Crying out, I held it with my hand and tried to push myself back up, ready for another blow.

It never came. I looked up to see the tamer standing over me. He reached out and grabbed me by the shoulders. His huge, coarse hands that I dared not struggle against were gentle, they rubbed me. With smiling eyes and mouth, he said, 'My name is not the tamer just as yours is not Caliban. My name is William Trask, and these men are not for fighting, they are our friends.'

He let me go and I sat against the bank, blood slowing in my veins. My back was sore and I returned to rubbing it now that my arms were free. The tamer struggled to lower himself beside me, groaned as he did so. 'My name is William Trask and I'm starting to feel like an old man,' he said.

My eyes began to adjust to the glow of the burning drum, and I saw the other men were smiling. Now that I had calmed they took steps towards me, talking amongst themselves as they did.

'It's Caliban,' one said.

'A personal show up close like that, I can't believe it,' said another.

William explained that the men were homeless, that beneath the bridge was their bed for the night, and that they had taken him in.

'But the whole town is after you,' I said. 'If the priest sent me here he will send them.'

'No one is after me,' he said. 'I went straight to the church after I left the circus. I'd never felt so clear in all my life, and that was the first place I thought of. I was baptised anew with clarity, I left that hellish pit and was drawn to the light like a moth. It was the priest who told me about these gentlemen, after I said I needed another drink.'

'It's a trap.'

'We've left the trap behind, now. You are not hated, you are loved. There is not a man, woman or child in this town, or any other, who hasn't heard of Caliban. Not one who doesn't love and admire you, my boy. You are *their* Caliban.'

'It's true,' said the other men in unison.

'You're a household name,' said one, 'and our house is the whole world.'

'That must be wonderful,' I said. 'I would like my home to be so free.'

'We haven't a door to close on you.'

They handed me beer, a drink I'd never tried before. It tasted bitter, and they laughed when I scrunched up my face. Around the fire they introduced themselves to the clowns and I, and William Trask talked.

27

Two years before William's last stand the circus travelled into a forgettable town in a country that may have been this one or may have been any. It arrived there as it always did, in the middle of the night, leaving a trail of flyers behind it. They made no mention of Caliban, but did of others. They mentioned the clowns, 'the fantastic antics of Pockets and Tick', they said, two faces as old as they look today. Bears and other animals, too. Acrobats and contortionists. But no Caliban.

I was alive, yes, but not there. Nor, as I dreamt, sleeping deep beneath the ground, curled up in a ball. Not beneath the nourishing earth, sweetly waiting to be thrust up and screaming through the ground's mud-membrane. I was at home with my parents when the circus came to that town. I will never know who they were or where they lived, only that they existed.

I was around twelve years old, I suppose, when my young family came to see the show. They sat on the lowest bleachers, right at the rim of the ring, my father on the left of me, my mother on the right. William was there, too, celebrating his thirtieth year with the circus. Very few had been there longer. He celebrated by wondering whether he'd die there, with or by the bears.

It was a wonderful show, he told me. My parents must have loved it, as everyone gave every act a standing ovation. Even me, I suppose. I must have joined in the applause. The clowns, though old, were sprightlier in their capers. The bears were younger and greater in numbers. The master was the same in every way.

When it happened he was under spotlight giving his farewell speech, persuading his audience to please return, to please sample the delights in the stands outside. He turned to leave the stage, applause mounting on his back, and the walls went up in flames.

No one knows what caused the fire; a casual cigarette dropped, perhaps even by my father; a mistimed firework went off, but it began at the base of the tent's canvas skin, spreading up to the rafters quickly so that the thing became a cage of light and fire and smoke.

To those beneath the tent that night a circus had only ever been a place of joy, no hint to the horrors that so often went on inside the master's. But, like any joy, horror is only a matter of perspective away. Theirs could not help but be fixed on a roof and wall of flames, when just a moment before they never dreamt of glancing away from entertainment.

Some escaped the blaze. The master, most definitely, and all his acts who were scattered about the aisle in safety. Slipping out through a rip in a burning curtain of melting colour, some of those at the back of the tent got out before it began to collapse. For the rest, flaming chunks of rafter fell to earth like wooden meteors. Smoke filled the remaining space, and the tent's frame began to wobble.

'Turn on the music,' the master was heard to shout, wanting something to cover the screams of the people trapped inside. Perhaps he wanted to keep the illusion of a show, as if that were its grand finale. A slow waltz started up, and a lucky few watched in the heat and the music.

The flames turned everything they touched, for an instant, a fierce yellow, then a black indistinguishable from the night beyond. There was a moment, said those who watched, when every inch of the tent was ablaze, like the sun had crashed to earth in revenge for its love affair with the night.

There was a second, they also said, right before the tent collapsed, when all the screams of all those trapped inside could be heard at once, when everyone wailed in unison. Just as the roof fell in on them, they had all begun to shout. Just as they took their last breath, that sad, beached sun went out.

This was the biggest disaster to ever befall the circus. Its inhabitants had known tragedy, some far worse than fire, but not one that had taken so many lives. Those not too fussy or too hurt helped clear up the devastation, and vowed never to speak of it again. The clowns stayed away. They had drunk so much after the fire that they didn't remember the event at all, just a bright spot in their memory. They stayed in their trailer feeling sad and confused.

The master, already inclined to seclusion and severity, showed no change of character, perhaps darkened a little. He had a new tent made and ordered the show back on the road soon after.

William helped clear up the mess. With him were the few surviving townspeople, a handful of his co-workers, and servicemen drafted in from neighbouring towns. It took them a week to extract the most of the bodies, and another to clear away the charred wooden beams and the vague, seared shapes of this and that. Amongst the wreckage they found melted jewellery, props, clothes, and things burned unrecognisable. The sand from the ring had turned to beads of glass.

On the fifth day of extracting bodies they found me. William and Leopold lifted a fallen beam from among the rubble. It still smouldered, and they dropped it fast after feeling its heat, their gloves already black and burnt through in places. It broke up as it hit the ground, throwing a cloud of ash into the air that sent the men coughing into their fists and turning away.

When the ash settled they saw me lying where the beam had been, trapped under it for days, appearing as dead as any other body they'd found. My skin was a sea of molten lava, encrusted with sand and grit and shards of wood. It was pulled tightly over my tiny body, and I lie curled up in a ball. When they laid me out and pulled me flat, large sheets of flesh peeled from my torso and travelled with my arms and legs. I had no ears, no nose, no lips. I didn't move, didn't think. Only a faint pulse kept them from burying me with the others.

'Now is not the time for mourning,' the master had said to William. 'I want the bears on the truck.'

'They're still a little spooked,' he replied.

'And I'm still losing money. Get the bears in their truck and get going.'

The master travelled with me in the darkness of an old trailer kitted out with basic medical equipment. With Leopold he worked on me for weeks, keeping blood running through my veins, treating my burns and waiting for me to wake up. William had brought me there, and assumed I died in that windowless room, but the master was the one who brought me back to life. Then he stuck a shackle on me, as soon as my eyes opened, and staked me in a dark patch at the end of his aisle of acts.

28

I was not born of the ground, but pulled from it, rose not from the earth, but out of ashes. I was a child of the real world, a world I have since learnt can be wonderful and kind. A child who died and was born again into a cage.

We all thought we were outcasts on the aisle, mutinied and mutant-like, that had found the only refuge for the damned. The clowns kept themselves in darkness, ignorant their whole lives to the world outside. An island of lost souls where everyone had turned their back to civilisation, saw in their warped memories only the evil parts. Those unable to cope with the tiny pockets of corruption that lie in every place washed ashore there. We needed nurture and help, but what we received was lies.

When I awoke in the aisle I was not a monster, I was just a boy. I was labelled Caliban, but that was not my name – I will never know my before-name. William was not the tamer, but had abandoned his identity, cast it aside at knife point. The clowns were not Pockets, not Tick, their true selves concealed beneath make-up, inches thick.

The master, as judicious an alias as could be, was not, I suppose. The assigner of characters, ruler of them, too.

Artiste of illusion, of incomparable phantasms. He appeared vengeful, but God-like nonetheless. He was in fact a magician, a puppeteer dancing falsehoods in front of the gullible. He lived behind the eye and caught the attention of those who'd stopping looking, convinced them with fear, with hand shadows of pitchforks and hangings. Then he ruled them with lies. We saw him as the lesser of two evils, a bad man, but one who'd protect us from the worse ones outside.

He erected walls around us, unseen barriers insurmountable to weak minds. When he built those walls we wondered what malevolent forces were being kept out. We were too fragile to realise that we were being kept in.

The world is all beneath a giant tree that throws its swaying shadows on a lawn. We must keep ourselves where the sun shines down, where it breaks through the leaves, as there are dark patches all around. William told me that the master had hung the three in the city. He had crawled into a penumbra and paid a man to do it.

Like the master, like the hangman, we had all been trapped in a dark place, but had finally broken free. With a new and cherished notion we drank beneath the bridge.

Over the night more men joined us, and were delighted to see myself and the clowns. They told us how much we were loved, and I felt a new thing, a daring optimism attached to my old yearning to leave and to explore. The future seemed more beautiful than it ever had before.

29

It was the next morning, hot and dry. William, Pockets, Tick, and I stood on a train station platform. The place was a tempest of new people. Some joined the train, others sat on benches, waiting. Some stood, like us, smoking and drinking coffee. Most had cases and bags. We had nothing at all.

The train was the one we had seen when we first arrived in the town, the passenger train so clean and comfortable compared to the circus' that had sat beside it. '*Express*', adorned the outside of every red carriage in golden letters. Its metal chassis was too hot to touch under a late morning sun which burned white reflections against its red. The windows were clean and revealed smiling, suited travellers reading, talking, and resting their eyes.

Dust blew in from somewhere, little storms on the hot concrete that blew intense for a time then spread and collected up against the red-brown brick of the station walls. Some piled around the legs of a bench on which an old woman sat and searched though her handbag slowly, staring into it with fixed eyes and full attention. She pulled out a mirror, patted her hair, and returned it with a sigh. Next to her a man in a suit held a newspaper.

I watched the station's clock move another tiny step towards midday, when our train was due to leave.

It seemed an appropriate time to dispatch ourselves from our old lives, flick like a railroad switch from discontented morning to brighter afternoon, to follow the sun as it would fall slowly through the sky towards a happy and free night somewhere new.

The clowns talked between themselves. Tick wrung his hands and shuffled about the platform. Pockets kept a hand on his partner's shoulder, and replied to his stream of questions softly.

They had taken off their makeup, had great difficulty removing it in the river where we'd spent the night. They were two old men, weak and worried. After Tick had his final questions answered the two embraced then watched the clock, both with smiles.

A girl played by herself on the platform. She wore a flower patterned dress that stopped above slim white knees, and had hair the colour of bottled honey. She chatted gentle as a breeze and flipped a folded paper thing about on the ends of slender fingers, counting to herself. She peered into the paper, smiled brilliant white teeth through her lips. She looked around, guilty at having this moment of solicitous and solitary happiness, then carried on shuffling and counting.

'What is that?' I asked her, and pointed at the folded paper between her fingers.

'It's a salt cellar,' she said. 'It predicts the future.'

'Can you read my future?' I asked her.

She smiled, 'Of course. Pick a colour.' I chose blue, and she counted off its letters.

'Pick a number,' she said. I chose a four, and she counted, 'one, two, three, four,' flexing the instrument in her hands.

'Well,' she said, 'that's interesting.'

'What?' I said. 'What is interesting?' but she didn't have a chance to answer. The station's clock struck twelve, and we were ushered to our seats. When I sat down I couldn't see her, and was disinclined to get up again. As the train's engine started up, and the wheels began their slow rotation I had already forgotten all about her.

I watched the platform from my seat, and saw a man point at me. Besides him was Leopold. His eyes followed the man's arms and leapt from the tip of his finger to meet mine directly. At that he jumped, span, and brought from the ticket office the master. Both appeared bereft of sleep. The master's wound had seeped through his bandage, and he dabbed blood away with his sleeve. He saw me, too, and the clowns, who had begun a panicked clucking, shuffling on the red leather of the train seats so as they squeaked beneath them.

The master and Leopold took off down the platform, reaching for our slowly moving carriage. Their boots on boards were inaudible beneath the metronomic, mechanical churning of the train's great engine, axes, its wheels on steel rails, propelled so entirely by smoke and sound it left them standing on the platform. The last I saw the master was panting, hands on his knees, while Leopold patted his back.

30

We had left William in the town. He was free to move around as he wished and he wished not to move from under the bridge.

'I'll make my way home soon,' he said, and gave us some money and clothes his friends had collected together. We used it to pay for our tickets, and I counted then the left over coins in my palm. I closed my fist around them and returned them to my coat.

Soon after leaving the station we crossed the bridge where we had spent the previous night. I did not see beneath it, but saw atop the houses the sun beginning its downwards climb. I saw, too, the fields beyond them that were full and green across the horizon except for the river and our track alongside it and two swollen figures that sat by the shallows of the stream. As we passed them I saw they were the last two bears. One pawed gently from the bank, splashed water upstream. The other rolled over on her back and scratched.

Lightning Source UK Ltd.
Milton Keynes UK
UKOW05f0848301014

240818UK00001B/2/P